Submission To Black

Blackstone, Volume 3

Rachel E Rice

Published by Rachel E Rice, 2024.

Submission To Black
Copyright 2013 by Rachel E. Rice
Book 3 Blackstone Series
Re-edited in 2023

Table of Contents

Prologue

I had planned to surrender to Mr. Black's wishes, raise the white flag, and marry him. I couldn't stand one day more of being without my son and Mr. Black. I wanted to shout, "I submit. Take me and do what you will. I'm yours." But something deep inside my soul made me feel empty, like a river in a dry season.

"This is not me," I murmured. This is not Alexander Bishop. I refused to be controlled by Max or any man.

I'd inadvertently stumbled into Maximilian Blackstone's world of control, excess, and secrets, and I'd discovered that I was not equipped to handle it all. I had no more energy to defy him. I was heading in the direction of submission if I couldn't find the will to control my urges for that devastatingly erotic, handsome man.

Chapter 1

Reaching and placing my head on Blake Scotto's strong chest was automatic. I didn't know why I did it. Maybe it was because his broad shoulders reminded me of my father's comforting chest, which was always welcome when I was a child. I could count on it to soak up my tears when I fell off of my bike and skinned my knees, and when I needed a good cry. Nevertheless, it was a mistake crying to another man when the incomparable Mr. Black was so close.

I learned that I had made a giant mistake when Blake placed his arms around me, cradling and pulling me into him. I felt his longing and desire, his heart beating like thunder breaking. I gave myself over to the warmth coursing through me, but this was not the time or place.

The jolt I felt wasn't from Blake, but was from Max's presence—his green eyes glaring at me. I jerked around, surprised to see him standing in the doorway. I stepped out of the warmth of Blake's arms into Max's cold stare, which riveted my body.

"I hope that hiring you, Mr. Scotto, was not a mistake. You are supposed to find my son, and here I discover that you are seducing and kissing my wife." Max stepped closer to me and placed his hand behind my neck. A chill leapt down my spine, settling in the small of my back. I wondered if he had used those large hands to strangle his fiancée. I pulled away. "I'm not your wife, and Blake wasn't kissing me."

"Then what the fuck was he doing?" he said, tilting his head to the right. Max took a defiant stance, opening his long legs to gain balance. His hooded eyes and creased brow displayed anger, like a wolf showing his teeth before he pounced and attacked his prey.

"I can speak for myself, Alex," Blake stated, moving farther away from me. Max didn't wait for an explanation.

"She's my fiancée, and you will address her either as Ms. Bishop or Ms. Blackstone. I didn't employ you to—"

"Mr. Blackstone, you can dismiss me, but I came here to do a job, and you know there is no one better at this than me. All I'm concerned about is finding your son. This is not about me or Alex... Mrs. Blackstone." Blake raised his hands and extended a folder, dropping it on the granite counter in front of Max. Before the folder hit the counter, I thought Max would hit him, or Blake would hit Max.

They stood glaring at each other until Blake opened the folder, and said, "Look, these are copies of pictures from your surveillance cameras." He lined them all up according to time and date. Among the many pictures appeared to be images of Max wearing a blue denim shirt, jeans, and boots, looking handsome and rugged. I'd never seen Max dressed casually. I peered at the photo, and the handsome hunk took my breath away. He was smiling and holding Maxim's little hand. They looked so happy together. It was a Mayberry moment. Why hadn't I seen that side of him before? But it wasn't Max's moment.

Max clutched the photo in one hand, his eyes drew tight, and he raked his fingers through his hair. "He's my brother." The pictures showed Jonas holding Maxim's hand. Jonas had a fishing pole and a large backpack with camping gear strapped to his back.

Blake raised an eyebrow, bit his lip, and shot a hostile glance at Max. "This information about a brother was concealed. Your staff never mentioned a brother," Blake said, angry and confused. "We would have been further along if someone had said something, Mr. Blackstone. You people with your money and secrets." I raised an eyebrow and peeked at Max's face. He didn't care for Blake, but he wouldn't let his feelings cloud his judgment and interfere with Blake finding our son.

"They were instructed not to disclose that I had a brother," Max said, pouring himself a cup of coffee. "We're identical twins. It was a business decision." He met Blake's eyes.

"Then, how did you expect anyone to come to the right conclusions?"

"That's why I hired you. You have a reputation. You can get to what matters without causing an uproar and making this into a circus, which would endanger my son's life."

Blake understood. It was a smart move.

"Do you know where he is?" Max stared into a cup of black coffee, twirling the spoon around the edges. He placed it on the counter, put the cup to his lips, and then drank. He raised his eyes.

"I think I know. Well, I have a good idea. There is a camping ground our father brought us to when we were children. There's a stream nearby. That's probably why Jonas had a fishing pole."

"Do you think your son is in danger?"

"No. Of course not," he said, his steely look disguising his concerns.

"Yes," I said. Max cut a serious glance in my direction.

"Well?" Blake asked. "Is he or isn't he in danger?" Blake's stare went from me to Max.

I gazed at Max. "For God's sake, Max, tell him about Jonas's history." Max lowered his head a moment and began explaining about his brother being a troubled child and a runaway as a teenager, his tour of duty in Afghanistan, his drug addictions after returning from the war, and his diagnosis of schizophrenia. He explained everything except Jonas's sexual activities. Blake's eyes moved with a disinterested glance, focusing on me and then Max, as if this was nothing new. He had an expression as if he had heard this a million times. It was boredom that lived within the policeman who had seen and heard too much.

"Mr. Blackstone, I need to go over information immediately with my men to ready them for the search."

"My gear is ready. I'll meet you near the pines in half an hour," Max said, leaving the kitchen and walking in the direction of his bedroom.

He dropped his cup of coffee in the butler's pantry sink on his way out of the door.

I bounded behind Max. "I need to be there too," I screamed.

He turned quickly, facing me. "And do what, Alex? Get in the way?" Max said. He turned his back to me, slipped off his robe, and walked into his closet. When he returned he had on a pair of worn jeans that made my heart flutter. He was shirtless and held his red-and-black lumberjack shirt in his hand. He wore a pair of outdoor boots, the kind you would see in *Field & Stream*. When he put on his shirt, I nudged close to him and began buttoning it one button at a time. Looking down at me, he kissed my forehead and brought my face up with his hands, so that I was gazing into his sad eyes. My need and desire for him rivaled anything I had felt before.

"I want to go, Max."

"You can't. The place is too rugged, and it's mountainous."

I pulled away. "How can Jonas subject a two-year-old to that type of environment?"

"We were that age when my father brought us out there. We survived in worse weather."

"Yes, but he's my son."

"He's a Blackstone, and I know what's best for him."

"Like leaving him with your brother?" I questioned, raising my voice. If anyone was listening, they could hear everything that was said.

"I didn't know Jonas would be here," Max said apologetically. "He must have flown down in my jet," he continued, moving away from me. He paced to the window and stared out. His eyes focused on Blake and his men, standing in the open space steps away from the gathering of large pines.

Max turned with a jerk of his body.

"I'm leaving, Alex." He walked out of the room with me following after him. When he stopped, he and I were standing outside, away from the pool and into the trees surrounding the property. Blake and his men waited for directions from Max. Van Horn had Max's gear ready and handed it to him, and Blake and his men trekked after Max. Knowing that Blake was watching, Max turned and jogged back to me, grabbed me, planted a heated kiss on my lips. It felt as if it was a kiss to remember that he was the only man for me. It scared me.

He whispered into my ear, "When I bring our baby back, we're going to make him a brother." I looked at him with surprise. *Doesn't he know? Doesn't he realize how I feel at this moment?*

— ◈ —

I HAD FORGOTTEN TO call St. John and tell him that I had an emergency. Reaching for my smartphone in my pocket, I dialed frantically, because I didn't want to lose my position at his bank.

"Mr. St. John."

"Yes, Alex."

"I'm sorry, but I had an emergency, and this is the first chance I've had to call you."

"Nothing serious I hope."

"It's my son, but all is taken care of. Max…" I thought better than to include another man in my private affairs. Nevertheless, he was in some way involved.

"I should return to Seattle over the weekend and be able to start at your bank on Monday, if that's okay?"

"If you need more time, Alex, just let me know. I will accommodate you."

"Thanks, Mr. St. John."

"I expect to spend more time with you in hopes that you will stop calling me 'Mr. St. John.'"

I hit the *off* button. An alarming thought danced in my head. I had not planned to lead him on. *I hope I can straighten it out before it goes too far.* There was no way I could have a relationship with any other man with Mr. Black lurking around every corner. And since I was so in love with Max, I had been deaf, dumb, and blind—and unable—to view any man in the right perspective. My heart wanted what it wanted.

I was born to love Max. No other woman could endure his raw, erotic, sinful sexual pleasures.

———— ◦ ————

DEEP INTO MY NIGHTMARE an ominous figure stood at the foot of the bed. My consciousness felt the presence of someone, and my eyes opened. I couldn't read the expression on Max's face. It was not one of panic, but then, he never panicked. He didn't say a word, just stood looking at me. "What is it? Is our baby okay?"

"You have finally acknowledged that Maxim is my son as well. And yes, he's fine." A small smile crossed his lips. I jumped onto the floor.

"Well, Max, where is he?"

"He's sound asleep in the first room to the right. You can access it through those doors." He pointed. I glanced at the door that led to the room where Maxim slept and dashed into it. I leaned over him and saw that he was clutching a stuffed animal. It looked like a small deer in his arms. *Oh, that's great, Max. Give him Bambi as a child and then later, hand him a gun to shoot Bambi's mother.*

I crawled into the bed and draped my arm around him and kissed his forehead. He didn't move. I looked up at Max. "Are you sure he's okay? He's so quiet and so still." I touched his forehead. "No fever," I murmured, glancing in Max's direction.

Max laughed. "He had a long day, but if you're concerned, I'll call the pediatrician in to tend to him. He'll give him a thorough checkup tomorrow. And you could use one as well."

"Thank you, but I will see my own doctors. I'm going to lie here for a few minutes. When I leave this bed, I want to know what happened. Where is your brother?"

"He's in the kitchen. He wants to see you and apologize for taking Maxim without notifying anyone."

"I don't know if I want to see him this soon. I still haven't gotten over him masquerading as you and never saying anything to me."

"He was just following orders. Blame me, not him."

"Don't worry; there is more than enough to spread around. You have to take responsibility for what has happened and what is happening to our relationship, if you can call it a relationship."

"Alex..."

I shuddered when he put his hand on my shoulder. "I think we need to talk, but not here," I said, staring up at Max.

I kissed Maxim one more time and rose from the bed. I walked back into Max's bedroom and sat on the sofa, looking out into the wooded area. He sat near me and tried to hold my hands. My hands were cold, and he felt it when I pulled away. "You are so cold. Do you want me to start a fire?"

"No, I'm not going to be here long. If you can have your jet take me back to Seattle when Maxim wakes, I would appreciate it."

"You're planning to take Maxim with you? I can't do that, Alex."

"Clearly you see that he's not safe around Jonas."

"Jonas did nothing to harm Maxim. You have no reason to take my son."

"You promised me that you would give me time to be with him," I said in disbelief.

"That was until I realized the threat..."

"What threat? The only threat is the one with that out-of-control brother of yours... I have something to say to him." I stood and headed straight for the door, but Max stopped me. He placed his hand over mine as I grasped the knob.

"Look at yourself." I glanced down and all I was wearing was a revealing cami with string bikini underwear.

"I didn't have time to pack anything. I just grabbed the nearest things and threw them into my bag." I made an excuse for my erratic behavior.

"Here. Put this on." He placed a robe over my shoulders. He stared into my eyes, and I met and held his gaze. His head moved to my breasts. He sucked one nipple, and he growled with enjoyment. My hand passed over his toned chest and abs. I was losing this battle and was close to surrender when I put reason in front of passion. *I'm not getting anywhere with this stubborn man*, I observed. "What's the use?" I said, pulling away.

Eyeing him, I said, "What difference does it make to him what I have on? He has seen everything. It's like locking the barn after the horses have gotten out."

"I'm thinking about the servants. You're to become my wife." I placed my arms through the sleeves of the robe, tied the belt, and turned away. "That's a little premature with the state of our relationship." And I sauntered out of the bedroom, leaving the door open. When I turned to glance at Max, he was entering Maxim's room.

It took only a moment to come face-to-face with Jonas. He caught me off guard, because apparently he had expected me to be angry. My stunned eyes locked on his white T-shirt. He had the sleeves rolled up, the muscles in his arms betraying the hard body under his shirt; the tattoo on his hand, a small star between his thumb and finger, was visible. Now I could tell the difference in the two men. The details had escaped me. *Why didn't I see it before now? Because, physically they are so alike. Only a mother would know, you idiot.*

I appeared to be in shock at the gorgeous man standing before me with an incredible tattoo, making me salivate and wish his arms were encircling me. I gained composure of myself to prevent him from seeing how hot I thought he was.

"Before you say a sword, Alex, I want to apologize for everything. I apologize for taking Maxim on that hike into the woods. He's a Blackstone after all. We were raised on fishing, camping, and horseback riding in the wilderness." Jonas's apology was not a real apology.

"That's an apology?" I said, gripping the side of the bar. "He's a Bishop too. Is that all you want to apologize for? Because, it was very immature and selfish to take a child out like that and not tell anyone."

"I wasn't thinking."

"Precisely."

"Now that we have broken the ice, have a cup of coffee with me. You may find something to like," Jonas said, reaching for the coffeepot. He poured a cup of brewed coffee from the silver container. "You see, I'm not a bad person after all," he said, flashing those green eyes and moving closer to me, causing chills to rise on my arms.

I stepped back, and he stepped closer. It appeared he knew the appeal he had over women, more so than Max. It was Max's incredible sexual antics in bed that separated the two brothers in my experience.

I gazed into his eyes and saw the seduction that I was running away from, but I also saw a lost soul and someone yearning to be whole again. In Jonas's eyes and the twitch of his lips, he appeared to be a nervous wreck, and although I felt his pain, I could not let my son fall into his hands again.

"Jonas, I have nothing against you, but I can't forget how we met."

"I can't say that that was my finest hour. I didn't know that you and Max were—"

"Yes, I know." I cut him off, because I didn't want to relive that embarrassment again. That kind of embarrassment took a lifetime to wash away, and staying away from the person involved was the only way I knew to lessen the humiliation.

"I will be leaving soon and taking Maxim with me."

"Did Max agree to allow you to take Maxim with you?" *There goes that word again.*

"He can't allow me or prevent me from having Maxim." At that moment my feelings concerning Jonas went from hot to cold.

"That is not exactly the truth. He has custody of him, and he can do what he wants."

"That is enough, Jonas. This is a conversation between me and Alex." I didn't hear Max enter the kitchen. He just stood silent until Jonas inadvertently informed me of Max's intentions.

"It is now apparent that you are not going to give me your permission to take my son home with me."

"This is his home, Alex."

"His home is with his mother, wherever that is," I said, turning to meet his angry, hooded eyes. "I am not a child, and I am not one of your acquisitions. I had nothing when I met you. I never wanted anything from you but my son. Now I realize that you will not compromise with me." I felt weak throughout my body. "What would your mother say, Max?"

"She would say, 'Take care of your son.'"

"Would she say, 'Take your son from his mother'? The way you and Jonas were taken from her? Why do you think you and Jonas are so fucked up?" I saw the uneasiness and hurt cross their faces, and immediately I froze. I turned and ran into one of the bedrooms to call Charles St. John. Arguing with Max and Jonas would not get me anywhere, and staying around Max was getting too toxic.

After rushing out of the kitchen and into the bedroom, I searched for my phone.

"Charles. This is Alex. Can you send a plane for me?"

"I can do better than that. I'll send my limo to Max's estate in thirty minutes. It will take you to the airport to my private plane. You will be in Seattle soon."

"Do you think it's safe to take my son?"

"Alex, the only way to gain custody of your son is with a court order, and that's impossible now."

I can't marry Max, and I can't be without my son. I dropped the robe and walked into the shower. The door opened, and Max stood behind me.

"What are you doing here?" I said loudly.

"You know that I get hot whenever you are around me."

"How do I know that you are Max and not Jonas?"

His warm hands touched my breasts. He moved them down slowly and settled on my mound. "I see you are letting your hair grow the way I like it. Do you remember what I said to you when first we met?"

"Do you mean the fortuitous meeting?" His eyebrow arched. "Those are your words, not mine," I said, throwing Max off guard.

"Well, if that is all you can remember, then what about this?" Max wrenched me into his arms, his hands cupping my breasts. His head lowered, biting my nipples hard, the pain excruciating and exciting and pleasurable. My nipples rose like cherries bursting into his mouth. The pain only heightened my arousal. He made the most erotic sounds as he sucked each nipple, one at a time. His hands reached for my clit, and his finger circled it until I was moist and panting for air.

His body's motion, moving his hard penis into my mound and rubbing against my pubic hair, excited and aroused me.

Then, my common sense took over. We hadn't settled anything. It was like putting out a forest fire with a cup of water. "No, no, this is not going any further. You are using sex against me," I said, pulling from his embrace and running naked from the shower.

"And you are using it against me by taking yourself from me, when you know that I would do anything to have your body. Anything!" His dark gaze frightened me.

"If that is true, then let me—no, I will use your favorite word—*allow* me to have my son."

"Only if I know that you will marry me."

"I'm no liar. I don't know."

"I have compromised with you, Alex."

"You call that a compromise when you have all the cards, and they are stacked against me. I would call that a coup." I threw on a pair of jeans, a tee, and a leather jacket. I had my bag in my hand and set it at the door of Maxim's room. I crept near his bed. I kneeled and kissed and hugged him. Then I walked out and picked up my bags with Max behind me.

"Where are you going, Alex?" he said, his demanding voice reaching a crescendo.

"Where I can be rid of you."

"You will never be rid of me." My glance fell on Max and then I notice Jonas entering the large room.

"I wouldn't count on that," I said, eyeing Jonas. I walked past Max and out the door on wobbly legs. My phone rang. It was St. John. I stood on the front entrance and answered the call.

"My car will be there in five minutes."

"Thanks, Charles." I walked down the stone stairs and stood outside in the cool mountain air. I felt the chill whip through my hair. I was not ready for this season of winter with Max. I had been used to a warm season. I had defied him, and I would be in for the fight of my life.

Throwing my bag on my shoulder, I stopped farther down the path and looked back and saw both Jonas and Max staring at me as if I were a child that had threatened its parents with running away from home. Their expressions mirrored my father's when I left home as a teen.

My father had sat on the porch, and said, "See you at sundown. Mother and I will keep supper warm." That was when I was sixteen, a rebellious teenager who loved her independence. The next time I saw my father, I was twenty-one and bringing Maxim home.

It had taken five years for me to face my parents. How long would it take to face Max and my son?

I looked up and saw a sleek black SUV rounding the corner. It had the appearance of an armored car. The driver instinctively knew it was me and pulled to the edge of the road, where a small stream and trees could be seen for miles. He came to a sudden stop, stepped out, and opened the door. "Ms. Bishop?"

"Yes."

"I'm to take you to Mr. St. John's private jet."

"Thank you." I stepped into the car, and he closed the door. Apprehension surrounded me, and I became lonely and afraid, as if I was that child of sixteen again, suddenly faced with the reality of my actions. But I couldn't turn back, or my stubbornness wouldn't let me.

A text message came across the screen:

Max: Alex, Y have you chosen to desert our son?

Alex: I can't believe that u would word this text as if u were planning to use my actions against me. U made me an offer of marriage and insinuated that it was the only way that I could have my son.

Max: It was the only way I knew to keep u.

Alex: You can't keep me as if I am a business of yours. Even they go bankrupt if u don't put something back into them. U can't keep taking from me and expect me to love u.

Max: What can I do, Alex?

Alex: Now? Nothing. The next move is up to me, not u. U have done enough to me.

Max: Alex, that sounds like a threat.

Alex: Absolutely!

Max: Alex, where r u and when r u coming back?

Alex: I'm not. And don't try to find me.

Max: My cameras picked up u climbing into St. John's limo. I'm flying to Seattle now.

Alex: Who r u leaving Maxim with? Not that psycho brother of urs I hope.

Max: Jonas is leaving for San Francisco tonight. He has an appearance to make. Maxim will stay with his governess. His mother has decided to desert him and his father.

Alex: U r horrible, Max. There is no use talking to u.

Max: Alex, don't leave me. We need u.

If I answered another text he would probably use it against me. He believed in scorched earth to get what he wanted. It appeared impossible to win with him. I loved him too much and I felt that he loved me the only way he knew how, but he could not see that he was tearing us apart. His need for family was great, and if I stayed around him, he would probably destroy both me and our son if I didn't do something soon.

The chauffer handed off my bag to me, and I boarded the private jet at the private airfield. I spied two jets side by side. *I arrived on Blackstone's jet yesterday and I'm leaving on St. John's jet today. What irony.*

I handed my bag to the stewardess. "Hello, Ms. Bishop. Your cabin is ready if you would like to shower. The food and wine menu is on your desk, and your bed is available if you need a quick nap. If you have any questions, ring this buzzer."

I glanced around, searching for answers, not the nearest exit, because if this jet crashed there was no way I could survive. "What am I getting myself into?" I mumbled in a fit of desperation.

Taking my seat, I looked around and spied the cabin where I could take a nap. I had entered into a world of billionaires, and the only way to fight a billionaire was with another billionaire. I finally accepted my plight. I had become the pawn in this chess game of rich, influential kings.

Chapter 2

After eating and getting some much-needed rest without Max looming over me, I stepped off the plane and entered a limo, which took me to my rented cottage. St. John had the good sense not to insist that I meet him. *What am I saying? It's not about me. Maybe he has something important to do besides babysit me. Maybe he has companies to run and places to go and people to see.*

I was excited to be in familiar surroundings without the pressures that Max usually laid on me. I put the key in the door, and before it could fully open, there stood Joshua. "What are you doing here? I thought you were on your way to San Francisco."

"I called and asked your roommate, Crystal, and by the way, why didn't you tell me you had a roommate and that she was so yummy?"

"Yummy?" I said, giving Joshua a second look. "What, are you a candy maker now?" He appeared embarrassed and bit his lip. I knew what he meant; I guess I was a little jealous, because he usually heaped attention on me. Maybe I was falling into thinking that everything was about me, and clearly it wasn't.

"I was just saying that she is gorgeous." He reached to kiss me, and I ignored him.

"Where is she?" I passed Josh, scurrying in the direction of Crystal's room. I noticed the rumpled bed. Not that this was unusual for her, but it was a bit messier than I expected—pillows, sheets, and a blanket on the floor, and her bra slung around the headboard. I turned to see Joshua standing behind me, wide-eyed.

"She had to run to the drugstore for something." His voice was shaky.

"How long have you been here? No, don't answer that. I don't want to know," I said with a raised eyebrow. I noticed that Joshua had his bags in the corner of the dining area. One had been opened, and shirts hung out. "I would offer you a place to stay, but there are only two bedrooms in this cottage. And we know how you like the good life."

"I've already made myself at home. You see..." Joshua hadn't completed his thought when Crystal entered, looking like the fox caught in the henhouse.

"Hi, Alex. I thought you were staying longer with Mr. Blackstone, or did you go off with St. John?" Before I could gesture to her, she had already let the cat out of the bag.

"What is this about going off with St. John?"

"Oh, that's nothing, Josh. Besides, it is none of your business," I said, looking at Crystal, and then my glare fell on Joshua.

"Yes, it is," Crystal said before she looked at me and had time to think. She had an annoying habit of talking constantly.

"Don't you know that he's Max's fiercest competitor? They have been at each other's throats for years. You're playing a dangerous game, Alex," Joshua added.

"I'm just getting help from him. I have to do something about Max and my son."

"I told you before: you can't win this with Max."

"Well, at least I can even the odds. He will know he has been in a fight."

"There are some fights not worth getting into, and this is one of them," he warned.

Crystal had left during the first round of our conversation. She was a girl that just wanted to have fun, and there was no fun in discussing men who she felt she couldn't get close to. I had never seen her walk into the kitchen, let alone prepare any food. I had never even seen her take out a plate or a pot, but I did smell meat cooking. She stuck her head out, and said, "I've set the table, and your steak and potatoes are ready, Joshua. Just the way you like." The way she pronounced his name and giggled, I knew that they had been intimate. Joshua leapt up from the couch and glided over to the oak table in the dining area, where an arch separated it from the living room.

"I'll pass," I said, walking into my room and closing the door. I could only take so much of new love, especially since mine had soured and so soon. Lying around looking up at the ceiling made life a little clearer. I had peace and quiet to think. No sooner had these thoughts crossed my mind, I received a text from St. John.

Alex,

My driver informed me that you arrived without any problems, and you are home. I have this job lined up for you and all you have to do is show up on Monday. You will receive an e-mail shortly.

Charles

⎯⎯⎯◈⎯⎯⎯

THE E-MAIL CAME AS promised. I made a call to Montana to speak to Maxim. He wanted to know why I didn't wake him, and he said that he loved me and wanted me to come be with him and "Daddy." I explained that I had to go to work and would see him soon. He appeared to be happy with that explanation.

With more on my mind than I could process, I managed to wake up early Monday morning for my new job. I passed Crystal's room and peeped in. Joshua had made himself at home. I sighed because they looked so typical sleeping, her head nudged into his chest, not like me and Max. As I walked out of the door, I saw a sleek limo in front of my door. I walked down the stairs and made a right on the sidewalk, heading for my Volkswagen, but to my surprise the driver stepped out of the car.

"Ms. Bishop, I was sent by Mr. St. John. He felt that it would be easier if I were to drive you to work."

"Tell Mr. St. John that I can find my way."

The dark window slid down, and Charles St. John's face appeared. "I wanted you to arrive on time and be relaxed on your first day."

"I appreciate that, Mr. St. John, but I prefer to drive myself."

"No pressure, Alex. Do as you wish." He raised the window, and the driver entered the car and drove away.

I arrived at the bank; its steel façade and tinted windows overlooked Seattle's downtown. I was directed to parking for employees. I exited my Beetle, and the attendant gave me a faint smile. Driving into the garage I had glanced at the parked cars. There were no used Volkswagen bugs other than mine. There appeared to be every make and model of Mercedes, BMWs, Porsches, and Audis; it was a car enthusiast's playground. Maybe St. John was trying to save me from being embarrassed, but I had long ago passed the embarrassment stage in my life.

Losing that part of me was the most liberating thing that could happen to me, and as far as the car, as long as it took me where I wanted to go and brought me home, I was a happy camper. The car was the least of my worries.

I entered the lobby, with its old-world charm, which was the opposite of the outer building. The outside appeared to have been newly built, yet the inside suited individuals that were used to money. I had to check my clothing to make sure I was dressed appropriately. Thank God for a black suit and white shirt I had left over from working for Max.

Holding on to the e-mail directions, I entered the elevator and landed on the floor that said *Insurance*. After handing in my information at the front desk, I was instructed to sit to my left on the large L-shaped sofa. A young man of about twenty-five came in and shook my hand.

"My name is Sean and I'm head of this division." I introduced myself and bounded behind him into a large, impressive office. He was dressed in a blue striped suit with a light-blue tie. I glanced at his shoes.

Never had I seen a shine like that on his black bespoke shoes—that was, until I met Max. He probably had one of the high-end BMWs sitting in the garage next to my beat-up ten-year-old Volkswagen. He was cheerful and less formal when introducing me to the staff. Sean explained to me that I would have a mentor until I had adjusted to the culture of the company.

Everyone went about their work pretending not to notice the new hire. They appeared to be relaxed, with smiles to match. Although they worked in a highly charged atmosphere, where money was the commodity, they showed no anxiety.

When Sean brought me to my office, he introduced me to my mentor, Marianne Huntington. She was a woman in her thirties who had forgotten she was thirty and not twenty. Although she dressed in a tailored suit, the skirt was short, and her heels were about four to six inches. I was reminded of my employment at Blackstone. However, she appeared to be a go-getter and a woman who didn't depend on her looks for advancement. I admired her and hoped to earn my way, I explained.

"Ms. Bishop, this is your office. It is a bit small, but you have room to move up the ladder if you do as I ask and follow the rules. I believe in following the rules," she said with a pleasant smile. "You should dot all your I's and cross all your T's, if you know what I mean. Make sure you observe and pay attention to details," she said, gazing over her black designer reading glasses.

I felt that she was looking through me. I had overlooked the wording of contracts with Max that had a profound effect on my life, and I would be damned if I did that again.

"If you make a mistake in this business, this company could lose millions. A misplaced comma could cost you your job. So, if you value your job, you will listen to me, and consult me if something is vague or you don't recognize a signature."

After she had given me the usual speech that all newcomers received, Marianne sent me down to pick up a packet of paperwork for new employees and sign off on my pay scale. I was happy to be working a day job and not spending my nights in a cocktail lounge. *What other choice do I have?* I rationalized. The cocktail job paid more than most day jobs I was interviewing for, but that would not have helped me in family court with Max. Now I had a career that paid a good salary and I felt great about everything.

Waiting for the elevator to arrive, I felt a sense of euphoria and freedom wash over me. A careful smile slid over my face. I stepped nervously into the elevator, not looking around, and faced the door. The elevator was large and filled with men and women. I heard their chatter and the word *St. John.* Then I heard a voice cut through the bodies standing behind me. "Ms. Bishop, I see you made it, and by the look on your face you are happy to be working with our family."

I turned, embarrassed. "I'm sorry, Mr. St. John, but I didn't see you."

"I know. But you are happy to be in my employment?"

"Indeed I am, Mr. St. John."

"Call me Charles." I felt eyes appraise me and just as quickly averted their glances. One woman standing behind Charles nudged her colleague in the side.

A small smile crossed my lips, and I said, "Well, Charles, this is my floor."

I heard him say, "Have a terrific day, Ms. Bishop."

Before the door closed, I blurted out, "Call me Alex." And the door eased slowly closed. I caught sight of his handsome face, his blue eyes lingering long over me. He had chosen to let his staff see that he had an interest in me. That didn't put a damper on my day, but the call from Max did.

I picked up my phone without checking it.

"Alex, I tried contacting you. What are you doing now? My security officers said that they saw you entering St. John's private jet. Are you all right?"

"I'm perfectly fine. As a matter of fact, I haven't felt this good in years."

"What do you mean?"

"I've been unhappy with you, Max. You know what the problem is. I don't have time to go through this again. We have been down that road too many times."

"If you want me to change, I will. Tell me what to do." I could hear the desperation in his voice, but I had heard it more times than I cared to think about. Nevertheless there appeared to be a hollow in his heart that he could not fill. I would not risk trying to fill his need, because it would lead to an unending circle of circumstances.

"It's more than that. I want my son with me, and I need time away from you."

"Come back and we will discuss Maxim."

"I can't come now; I've just started a new job."

"Who gave you a job?"

"No one gave me a job. You see? You think someone had to give me something."

"Was it St. John?"

"I have to go, Max."

"I'm flying my..." I didn't wait to hear the rest of his conversation. I had to get to work, and I didn't need the bad karma.

Glancing over the papers on my desk, I was careful to read each one thoroughly, but before I could complete them, Marianne entered my office. "Are you ready for lunch?"

"Yes. Where is the employees' cafeteria?"

"Honey, only nerds and the seriously underpaid people eat there. Have you seen what your starting salary is? Anyone who gets up to this floor is paid an obscene amount of money. In three months you will be making what I make, and we are talking six figures, my dear." My eyes opened wide. "Now get off your pretty ass, and let's go to lunch." She practically pushed me out of the door. We climbed into the elevator with all the other seriously overpaid men and women exiting the building. Some of them went left, but we went right.

We walked one block west and entered into a lobby. Inside the lobby a large sign read, blackstone. "Are we eating here?" I asked, feeling uncomfortable.

"Yes, they have some of the best steaks in Seattle. Besides, you will not see anyone from St. John's businesses, because of the feud going on between Mr. Blackstone and Charles. I hear it's about a woman," she whispered.

"How is it that you brave the treacherous waters?"

"Hey, I like that," she said. "You and I are going to get along great." We sat at the bar. I felt exhilarated, so I ordered a glass of red wine at Marianne's insistence.

"We work hard, and we play hard. On Fridays a few of us will go out dancing and drinking. It's expected. It's our team-building night. Are you game?"

"Sure."

Since I turned twenty-one I'd had Maxim, college, and getting a job to worry about, which left little time for anything else. Now was the time to enjoy my life, but the guilt of leaving my child with my parents and not disclosing who the father was weighed heavily on my conscience. There was freedom in disclosure, but not peace. Since Max discovered that he was the father, my life felt as if I had fallen into a cauldron of boiling water.

A waiter showed us to a table, where he promptly brought our drinks. Marianne had an infectious personality and was a regular there, and she knew everyone from the bartender to the busboys. I wasn't sure whether she had invited me to garner deep, dark secrets for Charles, or if she was just trying to be kind to the new hire at Charles's command.

Marianne loved wine, and she ordered from the wine list, an expensive, decadent wine that cost plenty and was sure not to get us drunk no matter how many drinks we consumed, she assured me.

After the first glass was poured and I watched Marianne drink, I asked her a question.

"Tell me about Mr. St. John."

Marianne looked at me and paused. "All I know is he is a damn-good boss."

"I heard he lost his wife."

"Yes, she was a saint. A beautiful young woman when she died. Not even forty years old when she got cancer. He was such a wreck when that happened. His hair turned gray. He became a recluse for a time. That was four years ago. For such a virile and attractive man, he never tried to date or marry again. I guess he couldn't find anyone to replace her. Until now, I hear."

"What do you mean?"

"I understand that he is head-over-heels in love with a twenty-year-old. The gossip by the cooler is that he met her in his restaurant. Can you imagine that?" She took another gulp of wine, and her steak and my shrimp salad was set on the table.

"No, I couldn't imagine that happening to anyone."

"It gets better. There was an altercation between St. John and Blackstone over this little waitress, and Blackstone left in a huff. St. John took the waitress home and has been seeing her since then."

"Really? Are you sure this information is accurate and not just office gossip?"

"Well, darling," she drawled, "You never can be sure. You know how gossip is. Believe half of everything you hear."

"And it travels on a fast horse," I said. Marianne glanced up at my comment, and then she cut her steak into small pieces, throwing a glance at me with each bite.

Chapter 3

Friday hurried along at a feverish pace. Learning the ins and outs of the job and forgetting everything else, I focused on what was important—keeping my position in this company. I hadn't heard from Max, which was refreshing. I had turned off my private phone and found some peace. I invited Crystal and Joshua for a drink on Tuesday and asked them to meet me at the bar on Friday, when the team-building night was scheduled. I hadn't seen or heard from her in a few days. She was obviously staying at Joshua's place, so I called her early Friday morning from my desk.

"Crystal, are you meeting me for drinks and dancing?"

"Sure, but I'm not sure Josh can stay."

"Okay. Just wanted to make sure you were there. I didn't want to go home alone. You and Joshua appear to be getting on well."

"He's a terrific guy, but he's leaving soon."

"Where is he going?" My heart began to race. As long as I had Joshua, I felt a sense of security. Now to hear that he might be leaving gave me a sudden headache. I wondered why he hadn't bothered to tell me.

I guessed I knew the answer to that question. Crystal had been taking up his time, and he was sick of hearing about me and Max. I would be too. That appeared to be all I talked about lately. There was more going on in the world, Josh had stated. We never talked about Joshua's life. Just me.

"I think he said something about King Kong."

"No, Crystal, that doesn't appear to be right. You are referring to a movie."

"Yeah?" Crystal said, still not knowing the difference.

"It's Hong Kong. Tell Joshua if he's able to stop and have a drink, it would make me happy."

In the background, I heard Crystal yell, "Josh, honey, Alex said to drop by the bar for one drink."

It was all set. It was going to be a night out with the girls. Crystal would meet me and Marianne. I had dressed in a short black knockoff of a Herve Leger dress. It fitted me in all in the right places. I grabbed a fitted jacket, so as not to call any attention to myself at the office.

Because, I wanted to have all my work completed before I left, I worked through lunch. I was famished and needed a drink at the end of the day. Marianne passed by my desk and stopped, and then she told me what I already knew, "You look tired."

"I'm more hungry than tired."

"Come to my office. I have something to munch on and something to drink," she said with a big smile, showing her straight, white teeth. "You need a full stomach for serious drinking."

I followed her down the hall and into her office. I hadn't expected it to be so lavish. Looking around, I was amazed at the space and the desk. She had a view of the harbor that I would kill for. She walked up to a mirror and hit a button, and a hidden bar moved around to face us. Under the bar was a fridge, and she reached inside and took out two chilled glasses. "Do you want beer or wine?"

"I'll have beer."

"Very well, but I need wine. I'm planning on getting drunk today. Oh, I almost forgot." She showed me a platter with a dozen small sandwiches and loads of fruit, which she placed on a large table in the center of her office.

"I like this."

"This is nothing. I plan on being on the top floor, right next to St. John someday, and you will probably get this office when I move up." She drank a second glass of wine and revealed her secrets of how she planned on moving up. "There are two more floors before I'm sitting on top of the world."

Peeping at my watch, I looked up. "It's time to go. I have some friends who are going to meet us," I said, cutting her off. Clearly she was ambitious, and she would probably reach her goals, because I had never seen a woman so bent on making it.

I thought my ambitions were lacking in the work department. *Maybe I should aim for the top. Hanging around Marianne could be good for me. Maybe some of that ambition may rub off.*

"Let's go, girl. I bet you have never been to a place the likes of the one we are getting ready to go to."

"Why? What is different about it?" I asked as we were walking out the door.

"Here. This is our ride," Marianne said with excitement in her voice, as if I had never ridden in one before, and she would be the first person to introduce me to the finer things in life.

"A limo? I'm tired..." I wouldn't complete the statement.

"It's St. John's car. I asked him to let us use the company car for relaxation and recreation."

"Why would he...?"

"Because I know where all the bodies are buried. Now get in."

As usual my selective hearing came into play. All I heard was *bodies*, and I thought of Max and the body of a young girl.

The limo stopped in front of a steel-and-glass building. There were no signs saying *Blackstone*, so I breathed easy for a minute. "What is so special about this place?" I asked, surveying the crowd. There were young men and women standing outside, waiting in an outrageously long line. We exited the limo and eased our way to the ropes, where the bodyguards raised the ropes and we stepped into the crowded entrance. I was following Marianne, who had the good sense to wear sensible shoes. My six-inch red-sole heels would probably render me incapacitated if I stepped the wrong way or on someone's foot. "Hurry. Keep up."

"How will my friends find us, or for that matter get into this place?" I questioned.

"I gave security their names, so don't worry, they will find you."

We were led through the building into one of many rooms and into a large room where there were individual spaces for dancing and drinking and smoking. Marianne pointed to a room to the side. "You don't want to go in there. Even if you see me enter, don't follow. You aren't ready."

"Ready for what?"

"That room is for the people at the top floor. It's only for employees that are in top management."

"You aren't there yet," I said, sounding like a complete fool.

We sat at a large booth and before we could order, we had a round of drinks; choices of drinks were sent to the table. "Everything is free. We don't have to pay for anything. It's part of the perks of working for St. John. Friday and Saturday we have this club to socialize and get drunk if we desire. No one judges. We work for different companies under St. John, and we all come together on these nights."

Marianne kept looking around as she downed a few drinks. With a bored look, I glanced around the room. I spied Josh and Crystal and raised my hand.

"I see my friends." I waved, and Crystal caught my eye.

"Great. I didn't want to leave you alone, so you just sit and enjoy. Remember, everything is paid for. I'm going into that room. Don't come looking for me. If I'm not out when you're ready to go home, then take the limo. I'll get home."

I didn't see which door she entered, and I didn't care. I wanted to see Joshua. He and Crystal made their way to the booth.

"Wow, this is great," Crystal said, swaying to the music and meeting the eyes of every man that passed near the booth.

Joshua came around and gave me a kiss on the cheek. He sat on my left, and Crystal sat next to him on the outside. "You look great. You even look happy with that smile on your face," Josh said, holding my chin in his hand.

"What is this about you going to Hong Kong?"

"Max finally trusted me enough to manage his Asian properties. I'm working under a mentor," Josh admitted.

"So am I. A very ambitious one," I said, rolling my eyes.

As we were talking, a guy came up to Crystal and asked for a dance. Crystal looked at Joshua, and he gestured for her to go. He looked at me. "It's not as if we're engaged, Alex. She knows the score, and so do I. We have nothing to bind us. We are what you call independent contractors. You and Max have your son. That will have you at each other's throats for years."

"Well, thanks a lot, Josh, for painting a morbid picture when I was feeling upbeat, and for me that comes once a year now."

"I didn't mean that. How about a dance, and how did you get here?" I held out my hand, and Josh took hold and led me to the floor.

We walked on the dance floor, and the small band and piano player banged out, "I Will Always Love You." It was slow, and I felt a sense of quiet and peace in Joshua's arms. "Where is your friend from work?"

"She left to rub elbows with the rich and not so famous. You know, the one percent of the one percent."

"I know my architecture, and this is one of St. John's buildings," Josh said, looking around.

"It is? I didn't know," I said, trying to be convincingly surprised.

The song came to an end, and we stood talking. Crystal didn't come back to the table. "I'm working for St. John."

"Doing what?"

"You act as if I'm not qualified."

"You are well qualified, Alex, but I never knew that you were interested in anything that had to do with banking."

"Well, I'm with the insurance side of banking. Billions of dollars come through my department." Joshua gave a judgmental look with a raise of his eyebrow.

"All I can say is, watch your ass, Alex."

"Please, Joshua; it's not what you think."

"It is what I think." At that moment, Crystal walked up and stood near Josh. We slid into the booth, and I ordered a round of drinks. I heard a voice.

"Is everything okay, Alex?" We all looked behind us, and standing on a platform glancing down was Charles St. John, looking handsome, all of six foot two with mingled gray hair and steel-blue eyes. He was dressed in a suit by a European designer, and no one could miss his taut body.

"Mr. St. John, this is a wonderful place," Crystal said in a breathless tone. He gestured and acknowledged with his head that he heard her. His eyes were focused on me, and then they scanned Josh.

"Mr. St. John, this is..."

"We have met," Joshua stated, and he stood and took Crystal's hand. Crystal stood alongside him. "I have an early flight tomorrow, and we have overstayed our welcome." Joshua leaned over and kissed my cheek. Charles glanced at him, and Josh gave him an ominous glaring glance with knitted eyebrows.

"It appears that your friend doesn't care for me."

"It's not you. It's men with money," I said, trying to apologize for Joshua's rudeness.

"I suppose he doesn't object to Max's money. He is being paid generously to watch over you for Max."

"I don't think Max paid him. He's a good friend and would do that anyway."

"Can I sit next to you?"

"You don't have to ask me, Charles. It's your place." I stared at him, hoping that he would sit next to me. I didn't like to be alone, especially since Marianne had deserted me and disappeared into one of the rooms with directions not to follow.

"That doesn't mean that I can assume that you would want my company."

"Why wouldn't I want you to join me? After all, you have been kind to me."

"I'm not being kind without a reason. A man like me always has a reason to do what he does. Take Max. He is enthralled with you, because you satisfy a need in him."

"And for what reason are you being so generous to me?"

"I have a need that you satisfy as well."

"And what is that?"

"You resemble my wife." Intrigued by his frankness, I leaned back. "The likeness is uncanny. We were childhood sweethearts. She had the same bright eyes and the same look on her face that you did when I first met you. I am taken with you to the point where I can't think about anyone or anything else."

"Mr. St. John, no woman wants a man to tell her that she reminds him of his dead wife."

"I know. Remember, call me Charles. You said that you like honesty, and I was trying to be as honest as possible."

I could tell that he was embarrassed to open himself up to a complete stranger, especially a man like him—extremely rich and powerful. It was a shell I could never crack with Max. I had to force everything from Max, and still, to the end, he was reluctant to come clean.

"I see you are drinking, Alex. Maybe it's time to ask you for a dance. Would you care to dance with a lonely man?" He stepped out of the booth and stood with his hand extended. I reached for it, and he took my hand. I stood next to him, and he placed his hand behind my back and led me to the dance floor. I felt the warmth of his body ease into mine. He looked into my eyes, and I could not look away.

His handsome, strong face brightened because of his light-gray suit and open-collared shirt, which caused the gray on the sides of his hair to glisten, and he looked so distinguished. I hadn't been able to see how handsome he was before, because I could not see anything or anybody but my Mr. Black. Now I was seeing Charles St. John for the first time.

Charles St. John was only a few years older than Max, but Max always appeared to have the weight of life on his face, and Charles seemed to be at peace with himself. That peace radiated to me, and soon I began to enjoy being in the arms of a man who made me feel as if I was twenty-three, or maybe seventeen.

He nudged his nose near my neck, and I flinched. I wasn't ready for a relationship with Charles. I had just started a new job that I liked, and I liked the people. I didn't want to complicate it with a relationship with the big boss. He didn't look like the kind of man that you could be intimate with and then take yourself away from at any moment without either of us going into withdrawal.

"Please, don't misunderstand my intentions. I want you, but I am willing to take as long as necessary for you to decide whether you want to be with me."

"I can't be with anyone at this time. I'm just dancing with my boss," I said as innocently as possible.

"Look around you. Do you see the stares and the smiles? Everyone is saying we make an outstanding couple." I hadn't noticed that all eyes were zooming in our direction. "My people know me. They know that I was never interested in any woman other than my wife. They know that if I'm dancing with you, then you are the one."

What does he mean, I am the one? I don't want to be the one. I just want to be. I just want to be happy without rich men controlling my life. I just want to exist in this universe, without all the nonsense. Is that too much to ask?

Finally, the song came to an end, and I could break away from St. John's universal pull. He took my hand, and led me from the spot where he had declared that I would someday be his, and back to friendly ground. I sat, and he inched to the side of me. He looked into my eyes and reached for my hand. I reluctantly hid my hand in my lap.

"Tell me something about yourself."

"Yes, Alex, tell St. John, and why don't you start with me." *Holy shit, it's...*

We both looked behind us. "What are you doing here, Maximilian?"

He moved to the front of the table, and my eyes grew wider. Was he going to expose me to Charles? "I was informed that Alex would be here."

"So, now you have infiltrated my staff with a mole. I wondered how you were getting information on me. It would have to be someone high up the ladder," Charles stated with an arched eyebrow.

"I'd say pretty high up," Max said, sharing a glance with me.

"And now that you are here, why don't you join us?" *No. No. That's the wrong move, Charles. You are inviting the wolf in. This is not good.* Max remained standing.

"How many times are you going to keep showing up when I'm with Alex?"

"You will see me as many times as necessary. Or until you just go away, Charles." His eyes bored into Charles, and he shot a mischievous smile in my direction. Then, I noticed that there was a small tattoo on the inside of Max's palm, between his thumb and finger. It was a star. I had seen that star when Jonas was drinking coffee. Standing before me and ready to sit was Jonas Blackstone, not Max.

"I have something to say about Max sitting with us." I turned to face him. "I don't want you to interfere with our conversation. Please go, Max. I'm sure you have heard the expression 'three is a crowd,'" I said, leaning forward and lifting my face to meet his downward gaze.

Jonas glared at me. "Only if you're vanilla." And he walked away.

Charles looked in bewilderment. "What was that all about? I've never seen Max walk away from anything. Did you understand the comment he made?" Charles, a man of the world, understood exactly what was said. He appeared to be checking to see if I had knowledge of what had been tossed to me. It was a ball I hadn't seen.

I hunched my shoulders like a teenager and pretended that I didn't understand what the hell he'd said. I was satisfied that I had gotten rid of Jonas, who had caused enough trouble. Because Joshua didn't approve of me dating Charles, and his position may have been in jeopardy, he had probably called Max to report on my whereabouts, and Max had sent Jonas.

Chapter 4

After drinking too much and eating far too little, my stomach rebelled. "I'll take you home, but first I need to get some food into you."

"Okay," I mumbled. I had never felt so sick in my life. Was it the mixture of drinks that my body, at less than a hundred pounds, could not handle? That probably was it. I was never one to drink, and food had always been my second thought. I could survive on tuna fish and sardines for months. That had been my diet when I ran away from home. I had loaded up on tuna and crackers from the pantry and stashed the cans and opener in my backpack to see me through my next meal.

"I'll let Marianne know that I will be escorting you home." He pulled out his phone and texted her. Helping me to my feet, a sober Charles marched me through the doors, shielding me from cameras. I climbed into Charles's limo, too sick and too drunk to care. I could have been abused in the worst possible way if Charles had been less than a gentleman. That was how sick and weak I felt.

My feet were heavy and my head light.

I woke to the sound of my smartphone in unfamiliar surroundings. I answered the ring. It sounded like the old-fashioned ring of a princess phone my mother once had. "I have to change that ringtone," I insisted. "Yes, who is this?"

"Alex, what are you doing to yourself?"

"Why do you want to know?"

"This is Max."

"Oh, hi, Max. What do you want?" I said in a dreamlike state. I thought it was a dream until I rolled over, and felt the sheets. They were

Egyptian cotton, with a thread count of over a thousand. I hadn't felt this great lately on my rough two-hundred-count sheets. I was not in my own bed. I looked around and saw nothing that reminded me of home. It was too luxurious to even imagine. There were no Monets, fake or otherwise, hanging on my wall with a little light for viewing. Then I glanced over to see a portrait of a woman who looked almost my double.

"It must be his wife," I mumbled carelessly into the phone, forgetting that Max was on the other end.

"What are you talking about? Did St. John drug you? You don't sound like yourself."

"No one drugged me. I am perfectly fine."

"I'm coming to get you."

"No, you are not." I sat up. "If you set foot on Charles's grounds he will have you arrested. I don't want you near me."

"Very well. I'll see you when you're home. And you can tell St. John for me that if he touches you in any way, he will have me to deal with." For some reason Max was fixated on St. John doing something to me.

Did he think that I would give myself to another man, because I gave myself to him with little effort? I would not make that mistake again.

"Max, you have lost your mind. Never show up at my home without an invitation. I have to go." I pushed the button and that was the end of Max. I felt great. One man willing to fight for me and another wanting to be with me, not for my body, but for me the person. Yet that didn't ring true.

Men don't fight for a woman's mind. They fight to have her body and soul. For now my body belonged to me, but my soul belonged to Max, and he knew it.

Whenever I heard Max's voice, or when his hands touched my body, my soul disappeared into him, and I waited for it to return to me.

There came a knock at the door. "Wait. I have to get dressed," I mumbled. I sat up, looking into a mirror across from the bed. I had on my short black dress from the night before, but my six-inch heels were parked near the bed. I hopped out of the large bed and opened the door. Standing in front of me was Charles with a tray of breakfast food and a bright, nervous smile.

"I'm going to leave the tray here, and when you shower..." I looked at him, dressed in a blue jean shirt and pants, and I thought I had fallen in love. It was just that I missed Max, and the closeness of another handsome man became sheer distraction. How could I handle this man when I could barely control Max with his insatiable sexual desires?

"I don't have any clothes to change into."

"But of course you do." He walked to the closet, opened the door, and pointed to the miles of blue jeans I could select. "See? While you were sleeping, and quite well I must say, I had someone bring in clothes for you. You can take them home or leave them here; it's your choice."

"I don't know what to say."

"Don't say anything. Just enjoy the moment. I'm enjoying you being here."

St. John left the room and closed the door behind him. Rushing into the shower, I spent half an hour trying to sober up from last night. *I had a wonderful time*, I thought, *until that pest Jonas Blackstone ruined my fun*. I gobbled down a small breakfast of poached eggs, yogurt, and toast.

A newspaper nicely tucked on the tray caught my attention.

Reaching for the morning paper, I spied the headlines: **DNA Results Suggest Tie around Heiress's Neck Connected to Maximilian Blackstone.**

I swallowed my water, coughed loudly, and choked. A picture showed the dashing, handsome, rich, sexy fuck, who I loved, sporting a wicked smile and a cigar in his hand. Where had they stolen that picture? I wished I had one in my bedroom. I tore the picture and article from the front page and slipped it into my purse. Then, it came to me: no judge in the world would give Max custody of Maxim.

That thought quickly faded. I dressed in a pair of jeans and a T-shirt. I walked out of the room and headed down the stairs. I saw Charles standing at the foot. "You are so pretty. I wish you would let me do more for you."

He held out his hand, and I took a step onto the marble floor. "You can start by having your driver take me home."

"Can't you stay longer at least until after dinner? You don't have to be to work until Monday, after all. It is Saturday, and my cook has prepared a wonderful meal. I don't like to eat alone. Do me this one favor for a lonely man."

Charles was a very persuasive man, and I succumbed to his charms. Before dinner he took me on a tour of his estate, and we stopped at his garage, which contained every car old and new that a man who was rich and loved cars could amass. We rode through acres of land, and then to the stables where he kept his horses. He stopped and stepped out and then opened the door for me. "My wife loved animals, and especially horses. Do you know how to ride?"

"I've never had the opportunity."

"Do you mean Blackstone has never taken you for a ride on his ranch? He has some of the best thoroughbred horses on that Montana ranch."

"No. I've never..."

"What has he been doing with you?" *All he has been concerned with is satisfying his urges for sex. I know he tries to say that he is making love to me, but that is all it was. It is what it is.*

"I don't want to discuss Max."

"I apologize. I'm sure you have unpleasant memories."

"Not at all," I said, catching and holding his gaze.

"Come with me." He took my hands. "You can ride with me, and next week, I will see that you have riding lessons. We can be together and enjoy the peace of the outdoors."

Charles was busy planning my life with him. I didn't want this to happen, at least not now. I needed time to deal with Max, but I needed Charles St. John as well. I guessed it was a quirk of rich, successful men to take over and control every aspect of someone's life, especially if you made the mistake of getting them involved. I had had enough of the controlling Maximilian Blackstone, and I wasn't about to hand over control to St. John.

"I'm going to be extremely busy for the next two weeks, Charles. Maybe we can discuss the offer another time. I think we should go back. I need the time to rest and ready myself for my job."

My hand stroked a brown horse with a white face and adorable wide eyes. Charles placed his hand over mine. "If you give me time, I could make you the happiest woman alive."

As much as that was a tempting offer, I couldn't figure out how to be happy with a man I loved beyond measure, so how could Charles make me happy? That had to be the best trick a man could pull out of his hat, but I doubted that he could do it, and I didn't want to invest more time in waiting for him to pull it off.

"I can't promise you anything, Charles. I hope you understand."

"I want... no, let me put it this way: I need you," he said, holding my hands and gazing into my eyes, making me weak. I wanted to be weak. I wanted to feel something for someone besides Maximilian Blackstone.

"Why me? I don't understand. You are handsome, rich, and successful..."

"I have all these things, but I don't have you."

"You are making me uncomfortable. I don't even know you."

"How long was it before you knew Maximilian was the one for you?"

"I told you before that I don't want to discuss him." I turned and rushed to the car. I closed the door. Charles walked slowly to the silver convertible and hopped in. He glanced at me a moment. I didn't want to meet his eyes. I stared downward, holding my hands. He started the car, and when my mind focused on him we were at his driveway leading to his door.

"Please, have your driver take me home, Charles."

There was disappointment in his face, but he didn't give a word of protest. He nodded and after a minute he looked away, and said in a low voice, "Whatever you desire, Alex."

———◉———

I MADE IT HOME. A SIGH of relief escaped my mouth. Charles was a man of his word. His driver took me immediately home. I lumbered through the door and found Crystal sobbing into her pillow on the sofa. "What's wrong with you?"

"Every time I find someone I like, they have to leave me."

"Oh, Joshua," I said, dropping my things on the table. "He'll be back. You don't need to cry over him. He's faithful."

"I know, but I'm not as faithful as him. I just might find a bum and go off with him and then screw it up with Joshua. I'm just like that. I don't know why I do things like that. I just do."

I put my arm around her. "I'm going to make sure that you don't fuck this up with Joshua. I love him like a brother, and I'm not about to let you mess up with him. So, dry those eyes. You don't want to look a mess, do you?"

"You promise. Promise me that if I stray, you will kick my ass."

"That I will promise." I knew what I was saying was empty threats and promises. No one could control a person's behavior.

Chapter 5

Joshua flew off to Hong Kong. He left us with our tears when we tried to make him feel guilty as he boarded the jet. We each had different motives. Crystal had found a truly honest and caring man, and deep down in her shallow mind, she knew it, and I couldn't bear to part with a big brother who wanted to see me happy.

So Crystal and I sent Joshua away and had our pity party along with a fridge full of wine that had been an unexpected present from Charles. It arrived in a crate, and by the name sketched on the outside, I knew I had never drunk such decadent wine before. The names were so French that I was sure even the French couldn't pronounce them.

We opened a bottle and found some cheese and fruit to imitate what we thought Frenchmen and Frenchwomen would do when they sat at a bistro and relaxed during lunch in Paris. I had always thought about going to Paris with the man I loved. I made a toast. "Here's to Paris and the men we love." We threw down another glass of wine, trying to get drunk and trying to forget our men. Sometime during our second bottle of wine, we heard the persistent ringing of my phone.

"Alex. Alex."

"Max, I have nothing to say to you."

"Listen, will you? This isn't Max. It's Jonas."

"Then I hope you don't take it the wrong way when I say I don't want to talk to you."

"I understand how you feel, but let me get this out. It's Max."

"What's wrong with Max now?" I asked, casual and unconcerned.

"Max expected you to return, and when you didn't, he set out in his small private jet, flying to Seattle. He thought that he could reach there before you. The last thing we heard from him was he was trying to land his plane in a valley. The weather changed quickly. I warned him before he left, but you know how he is."

My legs collapsed, and I found a chair. "What have I done? What have I done?" I said in a loud chant.

"Alex... Alex?"

"I'm coming there to you," I said, my mind in a fog.

"No. I'm going to bring Maxim and his nanny to you. Max's plane disappeared near Seattle. That was the last signal reported. We have a team of men stationed and ready to go. Just stay calm. I've done this before. I don't want to lose my brother; he's all I've got."

"You have me and Maxim, Jonas. Bring Max back." I couldn't believe my newfound feelings for Jonas. I discovered that comforting Jonas made me feel better. I found empathy for him, because the sound of his voice was like the lost child that Max had painted in my mind.

⸺⸺●⸺⸺

THAT AFTERNOON I WAITED in anticipation of hearing from Jonas about Max. The knock on the door felt comforting, as if Max would walk through and hand me my son. Instead of Max it was Jonas, as handsome as ever. Holding his hand was Maxim. Maxim turned to look at Jonas. He gestured for him to go, and Maxim ran to me and held me around my legs. I bent to pick him up, and he fell into my arms.

"Mommy. I get to stay with you."

"Yes you do." As I turned to show Maxim a room full of toys that I'd bought for him, Crystal opened her door. She stood silent. And looked at Jonas, who did not miss that where-have-you-been-all-my-life look, and Jonas answered with an I-can't-wait-to-fuck-you look. I stood to the side and watched the fatal attraction, which took me by surprise. I said, "Crystal, this is Jonas. Jonas, this is Crystal. And this is Maxim. My Maxim."

Maxim smiled at his introduction, but Jonas and Crystal just could not bring space between the two of them. Finally Jonas said, "You didn't tell me that I would meet the woman who would be the mother of my children."

"Oh God. Heaven forbid," I mumbled.

Crystal shyly broke a smile and held her hand out to shake Jonas's hand. "I'm pleased to meet you." Jonas reached for her hand and kissed the back of it instead.

"Jonas, please let Crystal go to work; she's going to be late." He turned and walked her to the door. I heard him tell her not to go anywhere because he had to search for his brother, and he would be back and hoped she would be waiting.

I took Maxim inside the dining area to play with the elaborate train set Max had sent before he decided that he should have sole custody of Maxim. Jonas stood staring at the door as if in a trance. "Jonas, what are your plans?"

"I plan to marry Crystal."

"Jonas. No. I'm speaking of Max," I yelled.

He jerked out of his trance.

"I have this team and we are going to hike near the last signal. It's hilly country with dense forest. It's cold out there. I don't want to alarm you, but Max left without a warm coat. It was as if he had lost his mind. I've never seen him out of control. He didn't think; he just rushed to that small jet and took off."

"Tell me you're going to find Max."

"I'm going to find him and bring him home. His son needs a father. I understand that more than ever. Well, we don't want Maxim turning out like me." A small smile broke across his face.

"There's nothing wrong with you, Jonas," I lied.

"Speaking of that, when I get back, talk to Crystal for me."

"You will have to do that yourself."

"I know I've been a nuisance, but I mean well. I just spent too much time on the streets and in Afghanistan. It makes for a lot of crazy shit."

"I know what you are talking about, Jonas."

"You couldn't have. I ran away from home all my life. It seems that I am still running away."

"I feel the same way. I was one of those urchins you see running around the streets of Seattle with nowhere to sleep at night, all because I didn't want anyone to tell me what to do." Jonas sat stunned, listening as I poured my heart out to a fellow lost child.

The sound in Jonas's voice had reminded me of the first time I realized that I was on my own on the streets of Seattle.

"It was a cold, rainy day when I decided that I couldn't stay with my parents. They were exasperated with my behavior. I argued with my mother and took advantage of my father. When they finally revealed that I had been adopted, I packed my things and stole away in the middle of the night. I had decided and convinced myself that I could find my birth parents.

"Climbing through the window with my backpack, my iPod, a can of tuna and crackers, and the ignorance of a child, I left the comforts of home.

"I felt deceived that they would wait until I was a teen to tell me. I knew that something was wrong. I just didn't fit into that family. My father said that I would get over my rebellious ways, but I got worse, and my attitude toward them became unpleasant for everyone. My shouting at my mother, telling her that I hated her, was too much for my father, and he began to pull away from me.

"Leaving home was something I had planned for a long time, but this time, I vowed I would never go back. They searched for me, but I didn't want to be found. One cold night I ended up in a shelter. I heard on the street that the sponsor of the shelter would provide financial support to any girl who would agree to finish high school and go to college.

"I ended up in Brooklyn, because I got a scholarship to Brooklyn College with an apartment and my clothes and food paid for until I graduated. All this help from an unknown woman. When I graduated,

I had college loans, because my last year, I lost my scholarship and had to pay, and I found out that my sponsor had died. It was then I met Max."

When the word "Max" slipped from my lips, Jonas's phone rang. He talked for a few minutes, and then he stood, and I followed him to the door. He turned. "My team is ready. I have to go, Alex. Say goodbye to Maxim for me. His governess will be here shortly. I'm bringing my brother back. Please, don't worry, Alex."

Jonas saw the strain in my red, swollen eyes. "I'll contact you the minute we reach our base," Jonas said to help me relax. He hugged me as we stood on the porch, and then he stepped down the brick stairs. After walking to his Jeep, he entered, looking back at me for comfort, then he pulled away out of sight. I didn't want to let him go, because he might be the only connection I had to my handsome, sexy, intolerable, demanding Mr. Black—a man who I couldn't fathom losing.

I didn't know if I could handle the loss of the only man I had both loved and hated.

Some might say, *You are young; you'll get over him in time*. There was no way I would get over a man like him.

Chapter 6

Nervously I tapped my pen on the glass-and-chrome desk. I couldn't get my right leg to stop shaking while I waited for a call from Jonas. Sitting at my desk all day and not eating, barely reading the bank statements, I looked up from the papers, and standing before me was Charles.

"What can I do to make you smile, Alex?"

"I'm okay."

"No, you're not. If I know anything about Max, he'll come out of this all right."

"You don't understand. His small jet crashed somewhere in the Pacific forest near a mountain range."

"You can't do anything here but sit and worry. I think you should go home."

"No, I can't do that. I have a lot of work to complete."

"Looking at your desk, it will take you all night. Go home, and Marianne will have someone take care of everything."

"I really don't want to. People are beginning to talk."

"Why should you care about what they're saying? This is my company, and if I choose to give a job to someone I'm interested in, it's no one's business but mine." Charles reached for my hand, and I stood. He led me around to meet his eyes. "I will have someone take you home. I don't want you driving around Seattle in your condition."

My phone rang. It was the call I had been waiting for all day. "I have to take this, Charles."

Charles turned and walked to the door. He glanced at me with his steel-blue eyes and gave a smile to light up my sad heart. "Jonas, did you find him?"

"We are at our base camp now, and it's getting dark. We will get an early start when it's light. I wanted to go, but the men suggested that it was very dangerous at night."

"What are those sounds, Jonas?"

"What you hear are wolves in the distance, and a bear."

"Oh God, Jonas."

"Tomorrow we can reach the site where the plane crashed. And if the weather is in our favor, I'll have Blackstone's helicopter and plane up searching the area." He added, "If Max is not in the wreckage, and if I know my brother, he's not waiting around for someone to rescue him."

"You said that he would be fine, Jonas."

"I know, but can't you see that there are no certainties? If it is at all possible, I will bring him home or his body."

"I can't handle this talk. I'm going."

I wiped the tears from my eyes, because I swore that I would not cry anymore. I would handle things. I wasn't doing that well. Deciding not to stay and complete my work, I stood up to leave, and I saw Charles walk through the door. "Come with me to dinner. I'm not taking no for an answer." He looked at my face. "When your boss asks you out, it is a good move to take him up on his invitation.

"Loss is a hell of a thing," he said, cradling me in both his arms. I leaned against his chest and was taken in by his strong arms and chest. I was just a girl again looking for solace in the arms of an older man. But this older man was by no way a father figure. His salt-and-pepper hair hid the youth and vigor of a thirty-something man who was eager to fall in love. Leaning on his chest, I heard his wild, erratic heartbeat, and I stepped away from him.

"You have found out my secret. I can't be near you without behaving like a schoolboy. I apologize. I should have controlled that by now, but there are some things only time can change. And since I still have a desire for the fairer sex, especially you, you should expect me to act that way when I'm around you."

"I don't know what to say."

"Don't say anything. Have dinner with me."

"I can only stay an hour. My son is waiting for me."

"That is enough time to forget."

There is not enough time in the world to make me forget Max.

"I want to assure you that you are safe with me and that my intentions are honorable. If I take you from Max, and that is my intention, you will come of your own free will, and you will tell me one day that you love me."

I could not open my mouth. I could not move. I was stunned by his directness and a little flattered as well.

"Well, Mr. St. John, I see that you have made big plans for me." I looped my bag over my shoulder, and Charles opened the door. I headed for the elevators, but he stopped and led me by the arm to a set of elevators I didn't know existed.

"We are going to take this one."

"Where are we going?"

"To my office. The view is to die for, and the service is outstanding. You need a distraction, and I can provide that."

We reached his office-slash-penthouse floor in a matter of seconds. Charles went through the double doors and into a large office area. Facing the skyline of Seattle with the Pacific Ocean clearly in view, I put my hand to my mouth to hold back the sound of amazement. I walked to the floor-to-ceiling windows and leaned forward, looking out. I had missed that view. I had missed being pampered. I thought that I could go back to living as I had before, but I was fooling myself.

I wanted to be surrounded by luxury. I wanted a man to wine and dine me, and take me to places I had never been. I wanted it all without knowing that I did have it all.

"Where can I freshen up?"

"There is a bath and shower for guests to your right. If you find that you need to sleep after dinner, then you are welcome to stay."

"I think I will need only a place to wash my hands." My eyes glanced at Charles. Walking to the bathroom, I closed the door and looked around in amazement. As much money as Max had, he was not as decadent as Charles. The bathroom was a mini apartment. The large step-down tub in the center of the floor was like a swimming pool and sauna. There were glass doors everywhere. I was afraid to open one for fear of what lurked behind it.

Wanting to leave Charles's secrets to Charles, I washed my hands and quickly left the bathroom. When I reached the room, an oval table had been set with a fancy white tablecloth. "I hear you love Chinese food and seafood. Well, you can have the best of both worlds." A waiter stood by, and at Charles's wave, the waiter, dressed in a white jacket, black pants, and white gloves, removed the cover over the tray of food and unearthed the delightful dishes.

"I'm impressed."

"Just for you, my dear." Charles reached for my hand and kissed it. How special was that?

Charles pulled out the chair, and I sat down. The waiter opened a bottle of white wine and poured us a drink. Charles held his glass out, and stated, "To the beginning of a beautiful relationship." Our glasses met with a *ping*. And then I heard my smartphone. "I have to take this, Charles."

I sat on the large sofa facing the skyline of Seattle. The lights calmed me. When I answered the phone, my heart was beating at an alarming rate, but I gazed into the lights and found my footing.

"What is going on, Jonas?"

"We reached the airplane, and as I thought, the fuselage is destroyed, but the cockpit is attached and somewhat together. But Max is not in it."

"What does that mean, Jonas?" Jonas heard desperation running rampant in my voice.

"Calm down. It means that his body is not there," he said before pausing. "But there is a great deal of blood. He could be anywhere. The blood means that he could be severely hurt, or it could be superficial. Max is a bleeder. If he got a scratch he would bleed profusely. I don't know."

Jonas's voice sounded calm, as if he had it all under control. He tried to hide behind his experience as a soldier, but I knew the voice of panic. The calmer he seemed, the more he became aware of the dangers Max faced.

"Jonas, bring him home. Bring him home."

"Don't worry, Alex, I'll find him. He's a Blackstone. We thrive on adversity. Look at me."

I felt somewhat better, but not by much.

"Alex, my team is setting out now. We have to reach him before the temperature drops, and with the blood and all... well, I don't want to alarm you."

"I know about wolves." It was ironic that I thought of wolves. I remembered thinking if Max was a wolf, as Blake had stated, he would be the Alpha wolf. I convinced myself, even if I didn't believe it, that he would be okay. *He will be okay.* I turned my phone off and walked slowly back to the table.

"I guess you won't be eating much tonight," Charles said, sitting quietly until I placed my phone in my purse.

"On the contrary, I need to eat something," I admitted. I tried to relax. But nevertheless, my mind was on Max, and Charles knew.

His glance traveled across to me, and I looked in his eyes. "Is there anything I can do?" he asked quietly.

"I don't think so." I lowered my head.

"I have all kinds of resources. I'll send a helicopter out."

"Max has airplanes and a helicopter out, and his men are searching for him. What can more planes do?"

"If I remember, he only has a personal helicopter. What he needs is the kind that has a heat-seeking device, the kind we sent the soldiers in Afghanistan." My eyes raised and met Charles's gaze.

"Whatever you can do, I'll be forever grateful to you, Charles."

He held my hand, and I presented him a warm smile as a thank you. After dinner, I said that I had to go home, and he offered to drop me there, but I declined. I kissed his cheek, and a glow settled on his face. He looked ten years younger. He could have rivaled Max for my affection if anyone could. I saw the handsome face that I hadn't seen before. Maybe it was his generosity to me, overlooking my love for another man, and that he was willing to find the man that I loved, which endeared him to me.

THE NEXT DAY I SAT at my desk and a call came in from Jonas. "We have him, Alex. He's alive, but barely."

"Where is he? Is he going to live?"

"He had climbed a tree before he went unconscious. If it hadn't been for an army helicopter, we would have missed him. We were camped below him the entire time. It had gotten dark, and we couldn't go any farther. A helicopter showed up, and the pilot announced that Max was in the tree hanging on to a branch.

"A soldier lowered a cable and was able to fasten it around his shoulders and pull him into the helicopter, and it took off to the nearest hospital. He's in Northwest Memorial hospital outside of Seattle. He's good, Alex; he's going to make it."

"I need to get there."

"I'll have a plane..."

"No plane. I'm going to drive. It's quicker." I hung up the phone and called Charles.

"Charles…"

"Yes, I know, Alex."

"I let Marianne know that I'm leaving to be with Max. Is that okay with you?"

"Of course. Take as long as you like."

"Thanks, Charles."

"Alex, come back to me."

I didn't know what to say. I owed Charles for Max's life.

"I have to go."

"How are you getting there?"

"I'm driving. It's faster than taking a plane and I don't think there is an airport for miles."

"Not in that car of yours," he said with a mixture of laughter and concern. "Take my BMW. I never use it anyway, and it has GPS." I hesitated, and he could hear my breath hitch over the phone. "I'm not taking no. I would drive you there, but you would refuse, so I'm offering my car. There is heavy rain, and I don't want you tooling around in that old car."

I could always recognize the truth when I heard it, and my good sense told me to swallow my pride and take his car. It wasn't like I was dealing with Max. Charles was a different person.

"Okay, but I'm bringing it back when I return to Seattle."

"Don't stay gone too long, Alex."

Chapter 7

As I stepped out of the building, a valet handed me the key to Charles's BMW parked on the circular driveway; I hopped into the driver's seat. Looking around to get my bearings and acclimate myself to the luxurious car, I stayed too long fidgeting with the buttons. Soon workers began lumbering out of the building. As I turned to check the mirrors, my eyes met curious glances from workers I recognized from my office. Their eyes narrowed and their gazes turned to one another, and they leaned in to whisper.

"Oh shit. Now everyone will think that I'm having an affair with Charles," I mumbled, turning the wheel. *He's not just any boss; he owns the bank, and he's a billionaire. There go my first and last friends*, I thought, letting out a gigantic sigh.

I put the car in gear and headed out, but not before contacting Jonas. I asked him to look in on Maxim and make sure the nanny was taking care of him. Jonas being a good sport and, I'm reluctant to say, a good uncle, agreed to care for Maxim instead of remaining at the bedside of Max. Jonas revealed that Max was still unconscious, but the doctors expected him to be lucid soon.

I couldn't get to the hospital soon enough, but I welcomed the drive. It was a way to leave behind some of myself. I pulled into the entrance where there was valet parking and handed the attendant the keys. I turned before he entered the car. "Take care of it. It's not mine. I can't afford to even pay the deductible."

The young man smiled as if he understood my predicament.

Stopping at the information desk, I asked for the critically injured patients. A girl about my age instructed me to turn right at the corner, and there I would find the elevators. I hit the elevator button.

Walking in, I hit the button for the eighth floor, the elevator stopped, and I got off looking for the room. At the end of the hall to the left, there was his room. I rinsed my hands and stepped inside. The nurse and doctors were walking out. "How is he?"

"Mr. Blackstone is doing fine. My team stopped the bleeding, Mrs. Blackstone. It was a superficial cut to the head. We gave him something to rest and we're feeding him intravenously. He had a bad night. Other than insect bites and a concussion, he will be fine if he gets some rest."

I thanked them and walked into the room and looked down on Mr. Black. I touched his hand and held it. He appeared to respond, but that was just me hoping for the best. It was strange seeing him so vulnerable with his head bandaged and tubes in his arm, mouth, and nose.

"Max, can you hear me? I love you." Tears fell from my eyes, rolled down my cheeks, and landed on his face.

His heart monitor went haywire. Then his eyes opened. "Alex, darling," he said with slurred speech. "I heard your voice and then something struck my face." He placed his left hand on his cheek.

It's a tear, you handsome fuck.

"It's my tear, you intolerable, stubborn, handsome man. Good to see you alive."

He managed to look up at me, and then, searching his surroundings with his intense green eyes, he mumbled, "What am I doing here and why are you here?"

Because I love you, you beautiful, crazy fuck. "You were in an accident."

"Now I remember. I headed out alone in my plane after I realized that you had left me."

"Don't talk. You need to sleep."

"Only if you promise me that you will stay with me all night."

"You bet. I'm not going anywhere." I took off my jacket and laid my purse down and held Max's hand. He closed his eyes and fell back to sleep. I guessed he needed it after what he had been through. A meal was brought in for me. The room wasn't fancy, but he did have the best room in this country hospital, complete with an extra bed and a couch.

At about midnight Max was still sleeping when my phone vibrated and woke me.

"Alex, this is Jonas."

"Yes, Jonas, how is Maxim?"

"He misses you and Max, but Crystal and I are taking good care of him."

"Where is the nanny?"

"I gave her a few days off."

"What do you mean? You and Crystal are taking care of my baby?"

"Crystal cooks…"

"I've never known Crystal to cook anything."

"We have plans to take him…"

"Hold on, Jonas. Where are you staying?"

"I'm staying at your house to make sure Maxim is taken care of."

"Jonas, don't do anything I'm going to be sorry for."

"Don't worry, Alex. I've got this."

"That's why I'm worried. I should be home tomorrow. Max is doing fine; he finally caught up with his rest." My phone signaled another call was coming in. "I have to go. Jonas, take care of my baby.

"Charles, I'm sorry I didn't call you, but I was tired."

"I just wanted to know whether you made it safely. That's all, and since I've heard your voice, I'm a happy man."

"Charles, I'll see you tomorrow."

"No, take another day."

"Goodnight, Charles."

Max stirred in his bed and asked for water. He appeared to be dreaming. It was a nightmare and he screamed for his mother. I ran to his bed and shook him, waking him. I wanted to cradle him in my arms and tell him it would be all right, but I knew he would resent me for knowing that he was not the master of the universe. There was a little kid hiding beneath his façade.

His eyes caught mine. He appeared embarrassed, lying in bed with no control of his surroundings, because my Mr. Black was a stickler for control.

"You were having a nightmare. You screamed for your mother. And then you had this look on your face and said, 'Alex, Rebecca,' and then you repeated, 'St. John.'"

"I thought I heard you call out to St. John."

"I was talking to Charles," I said, not knowing the effect it would have on Max.

"Why were you speaking to him?" Max said in a demanding, but weak voice.

I raised an eyebrow to signal my discontent with him. "Charles was the one who sent a helicopter to rescue you. And I would not be by your side if he hadn't let me use his car."

"You drove here in his car?" Max tried to lift his tired, perfect body. "Alex, you don't understand that man. You can't handle a man like him."

"I think I heard the same thing about you."

"I forbid you to see him."

"You can't forbid me to see anyone. You have my child, and now you want to control my life. If it wasn't for Charles, you wouldn't be here today."

"That's not the complete truth. I would have made it out without his interference." I didn't doubt Max's stubbornness and grit. He might have survived and made it out of that wilderness, but Jonas and I didn't want to take a chance on never seeing him again.

"Can't you admit when you're wrong and stop looking for excuses?"

Max turned his back to me. He lay facing the window, with his hard ass displayed through the gown. I wanted to snuggle up behind him and tell him that I would marry him, but two stubborn people were cancelling each other out. Something had to give.

The rain fell hard but not so as to drown out Max's words. "I want you, Alex. I want you to myself."

Could I trust my handsome, sexy man with the truth? Or would I fall prey once more in a moment of my weakness? Even after we made love, it didn't prevent him from exercising his will over me.

He's brazen when he tells me that he wants me. He's telling me that no matter what I want, he means to have me. I need to fight him to claim my son, my mind, and my body, because he intends on taking all of me, leaving nothing of me I can recognize.

"You had me, Max, but now..." He turned, facing me. *That face and body would make any woman drop to her knees and beg for one more day with him.* But I tried to hide my yearning for his incredible body. *What will I do if I can't have him?*

"I can change, Alex." He sounded so convincing that I almost relented.

"I don't see it coming soon. Since you are better, I'm going to leave in the morning." I walked to the bed opposite his, climbed into it, and watched Max close his eyes. He didn't want to admit how exhausted he had become and how exhausting the conversation was. *Max has to be heavily medicated for him to fall asleep speaking to me*, I thought. *I had better leave before he wakes and convinces me that he is the only man in the world for me.*

Waking the next morning, I saw the remnants the rain left behind—raindrops covering the windows and clinging to the trees, a dreary, damp morning. I bent and kissed Max on his cheek and forehead. He reached for me with weary hands. His eyes were like slits on his face. I stood looking at him. I could never get enough of that dark, curly hair, that strong jaw and dimples, that hard, rippling chest, and those dark, secretive green eyes. I wanted to stand there for hours and drink him in like a thirsty man finding water in the desert, but I didn't.

I slipped out of the room and out of the hospital and headed down a lonely stretch of road back to my son.

———◦———

I ARRIVED IN SEATTLE just in time to see Jonas and Crystal drive off with Maxim in the backseat. Because they didn't see me and didn't hear the blowing of my horn, I couldn't stop them. I needed some rest, so I took that as a sign to get in some much-needed sleep. Before I could run into the shower, I checked my smartphone and noticed that I had missed calls from—of all people—Max and Josh.

A text came in soon after. I blinked, took a deep breath, and then read it.

Max: Alex, y did u leave me?

Me: Max, r u trying to make me feel guilty? But of course u r.

Max: I miss u. When r u coming back?

Me: The doctor said that u r fine and u need some rest.

Max: I need u. I can't function without u.

Me: If u mean fucking me, u will have to find someone else.

I couldn't believe I wrote that. I didn't want him to find another woman. I just wanted him to change.

There were no other texts coming in, and I used that opportunity to take a shower. I stood under the hot water for what felt like an hour. I must have used all the excess water in the reservoir. Finally, I exited the shower, exhausted and ready for sleep.

Before I could dress and fall in bed, I read Joshua's texts.

Joshua: Contact me. Heard about Max.

Me: Do u ever answer ur phone or texts?

Joshua: Where is Crystal? I haven't heard from her in a week.

I owed Josh an answer.

Me: Josh, Max is OK. And Crystal is being Crystal.

What could I say to my dearest friend? *She has fallen for a handsome, rich psycho. I'm sure that wouldn't go over well.*

Joshua: I'll see u soon, Alex. Tell Crystal I love her and miss her, and to turn on her phone.

The thought of Joshua flying in made me anxious and nervous. I had to speak to Crystal, but first I needed some sleep. Lying across the bed with my eyes closed, my body went numb. I woke to the sound of laughter and the smell of fish wafting from the kitchen.

Throwing on a robe, I pulled my hair into a ponytail. Crystal and Jonas were in the kitchen, hanging over a frying pan and giggling. Jonas was standing behind Crystal, pressing into her butt, nibbling on her ear, and nudging her neck with his nose. He whispered something into her ear, and she let out a cackle, as if she was a hen who had just laid a perfect egg and couldn't wait to show it off.

"I hate to interrupt what appears to be a tender moment, but where is Maxim?"

"He's sleeping in my bed," Crystal said, turning with a smile.

"In that bed?" I questioned.

"Don't worry, I changed the sheets," Crystal stated, tucking her chin under as Jonas tickled her chin. He whispered into her ear as if I was invisible, and she let out a mischievous snicker.

"That's not what I'm worried about," I said, returning to my original thought. "Joshua called and said for you to turn on your phone."

"Oh, I was so busy..."

"I can see that." Crystal leaned back into Jonas. His hands circled her waist. She caught his hands and held them in a loving embrace.

Breaking away from the embrace, Jonas turned to watch me in the doorway. He reached for a cup of coffee, and there, between his thumb and forefinger, was the tattoo of a star, which confirmed what I knew. He had been impersonating Max at Charles's company team-building night. He was so convincing that Charles hadn't known, but then, no one knew there were two of them. It was the best-kept secret. But like everything in life, the sun would shine on that too.

Jonas reached for Crystal's hand and said, "Crystal and I are going to spend some time together. She will be staying at my place for a few days."

"Not that..." His eyes flashed at me. I read the darkness in his jade eyes and knew not to continue, as I had done when Max was angry. "You two have a great time. Jonas, I need to speak to you," I said. I was as firm and demanding as I could be without alarming Crystal. While Crystal continued cooking, I pointed for Jonas to follow me.

We stood outside of Crystal's viewing and hearing range. "What's going on, Jonas? She's vanilla in your world. Crystal is one step from milking cows on a farm."

"You were vanilla once," he stated defensively. "That didn't stop you from accepting my brother's world and falling for him."

"I'm out of that now. There is no going back to that for me."

He raised an eyebrow. "Why don't you admit it? You love what he introduced you to." His gaze swept over me, acknowledging that we shared a secret. He knew, and I had to admit it.

"I loved it because it was just between me and Max. Something happened when he sent me to Pandora's Retreat, and didn't tell me that I would meet you, his brother, and that woman who you sent to his room in Vegas. Frankly, I haven't been able to forgive you and myself for being so stupid. And as for that dead heiress..." I stopped cold because of Jonas's expression and body language. He raked his fingers through his black, curly hair over and over until he saw my eyes following his hand. Then he tucked it into his pocket to hide his nervousness.

"Alex, everyone has secrets plaguing their lives. If I didn't forgive myself for all the things I have done that I'm ashamed of, I would be dead or a wreck."

"You are a wreck. And you may have just begun to destroy Crystal. She is too young for you."

"You were barely twenty when you met Max," he stated, not expecting an answer.

"That's different. Crystal is a farm girl. I lived on the streets as a teen, went to college, and learned lessons in New York that made me aware of life. You have got to give her a chance."

Jonas turned with a solemn face. His head low and his eyes traveling into the distance, he headed for the kitchen. I heard Crystal say, "Food is ready." Standing in the entrance, I saw Jonas embrace Crystal from behind. It was a caring and loving embrace, and it was what I wanted and desired from Max, but he never stood still long enough to be my man in the kitchen, or to hold my hand and tell me he loved me, without sex being on the menu.

I refused Crystal's invite. I needed eggs, bacon, and an English muffin. I cooked after they exited the kitchen and sat in the dining room. Jonas and Crystal ate hurriedly and brought the dishes back into the kitchen to lay them in the sink. "I'll wash them. No dishwasher," I said, looking up at Jonas.

"I'll send one," Jonas said, smiling at Crystal. He was caught up with the allure of a fresh body.

Crystal smiled at him. "Alex doesn't want a dishwasher. She likes doing the dishes. Me, I hate it—too many brothers and too many dishes." She dropped the plates in the sink, and she and Jonas strutted out holding hands.

Turning, Jonas met my gaze. "Crystal and me, we're going to my place. I have an apartment downtown." I looked curiously at him. "Max is never there." He hunched his shoulders. "Spend some time with Maxim before I bring him back to Montana."

"I thought I would have him with me until Max was released from the hospital."

"His doctors released him this morning. They said that he could recuperate at home in Montana. He called me and said to bring his son home. He's angry with you for leaving."

"What else is new?" I said, staring at Jonas. "Did he say any more?"

"No. I'm sorry, Alex."

"What do you mean you're sorry?"

"Just that. I meant nothing by it."

"Is there something you're not telling me, Jonas?" I grabbed his arm, wheeling him around.

"I told you everything I know. I'll be back to get Maxim tonight at eight," he stated with a dismissive stare.

Chapter 8

Jonas took Maxim and brought back Crystal. It wasn't a fair exchange. When I woke the next morning, Crystal lay snug in her bed. Good thing she hadn't quit her day job, because Jonas was not a man you could depend on; but I didn't have time to tell her that, and I didn't want to be the messenger of bad news.

I drove Charles's car to the front of the bank, and a valet hopped in and drove it away. Walking slowly, I entered the building and let out a contented sigh. I was excited about losing myself in my work. I knew little about the insurance side of banking. Marianne guaranteed me that with her help, I would be a fierce businesswoman in no time. All I had to do was follow her lead, not ask too many questions, and go to all of the meetings and keep my mouth shut. In other words, "Fake it until you make it."

I knew that I could do that for now. Especially the part about not asking many questions and keeping my mouth shut. I didn't know enough to know what questions to ask. Sitting at my desk and reviewing the papers from the day before, I began checking everything to make sure the signatures matched and that the individuals signing the checks were who they said they were. It was lunchtime, and I hadn't heard from Charles. I picked up the phone to call him and tell him that I had brought his expensive BMW back without a scratch and that I was thankful.

I had been concentrating on my work, and I didn't see a woman come through the door. Glancing up, I caught sight of a cold, stiff expression. Standing in front of my desk was an unfamiliar yet familiar face. I placed the phone down and met her eyes. The young woman wore a very expensive cream-colored wool-and-silk suit, no jewelry except for a pair of canary-yellow diamond earrings. It occurred to me that Max loved to give presents of yellow diamond jewelry. At a distance she could resemble me, only her hair was straight and dark, set against flawless porcelain skin. She had a pair of shiny dark eyes that glared down at me.

She stood in front of my desk with an expensive purse at her side, and said, "I'm looking for Alexander Bishop." Peering at my nameplate and then meeting my eyes, she drawled, "Oh, that's you." She touched my nameplate in a curious manner.

"I thought that you would be prettier," she said, turning up her nose with a sneer and glaring at my office furniture.

"And who are you?" I said, surprised by the unsuspected attack launched at me.

"I'm the woman who's going to marry Maximilian." I sat up and straightened my skirt out of nervousness.

"If you are marrying him, then why do you find it necessary to give me this bit of information?" I said, standing to gain control of the situation. "Would you like something to drink, Miss, uh...what did you say your name—" She cut me short.

"Ms. Beaumont. Jessica Beaumont," she said with ringing emphasis and a pretense of wealth and good breeding. She sat down in the chair opposite my desk and left me standing. I walked to my fridge and retrieved a bottle of water. I held up the bottle and pointed it at her, but she shook her head no.

When I reached my desk to sit, she said, "I didn't come here to drink or exchange pleasantries with you. I wanted to inform you that whatever you had with Maximilian is over."

"Don't you think that's up to Max to decide?" I said with control of my voice, showing a cool gaze to temper the heat of her black eyes.

"Max is confused, and he's all caught up with his son. He doesn't know what's good for him, but that will change."

"And you do, Miss, uh—" She cut me off.

"Beaumont. I'm sure Max has spoken of me," she said with a haughty manner and her head held high. It was as if she had been rehearsing to affect a classy demeanor she had read about or seen somewhere, but clearly it wasn't a natural state for her.

"I never heard him speak your name. I saw you at his fundraiser, but that was after I refused to accept his invitation." I glanced her way, gauging her reaction. "And did Max tell you where he went when he left the podium?" Her eyes grew wide. Not waiting for her to reply, I said, "He was with me, and we were enjoying each other's bodies. Do I have to draw you a picture?" By the slits her eyes made, and the biting of her lip, she had created a better picture in her mind than words could conjure.

I refused to let him fuck me until he came clean about the strangled woman, which he never did. A small lie is good for the soul and good for a bitch like you, Ms. Beaumont, I thought.

"We have a history together, Ms. Bishop. My family raised Max and his brother. Max and I have been lovers since we were teenagers." She measured my gaze and body language. I gave nothing away in my expression, but I felt like shit. She continued after staring me down, "I taught him everything he knows. Maybe some of what he used on you." Her head tilted left, and a wicked smile crawled across her face. "You can thank me for your orgasms. I taught him how to satisfy me with oral sex," she said with a deliberate voice. My eyes closed and opened as if I expected her to disappear. "I have an investment in him." She raised her voice. "Do you think I will stand by while another woman takes what I want and what I enjoy?" Her riveting eyes bored into me.

That bit of information had me reeling. *Why didn't my Mr. Black tell me that a psychotic woman was fighting me for his affections?*

I focused my attention and rage on her. "Your parents did a very poor job of raising them, I hear. And as for the orgasms, since it was Max who satisfied me with his tongue, fingers, and body, and not you, I'll reserve that credit for him."

All my animosity for her and for what Max hadn't told me flashed across my face. "Why would he marry you when all I have to do is call him and I can have him any way and anytime I desire? Did he tell you how and when we make love? Or did he tell you how I suck his dick and make him come whenever I want!"

I'm keeping a scorecard, Jessica, and you have lost this round, you cunt.

"You are a bitch," she said with as much force as those words could command.

"Yes, and a better one than you, Ms. Beaumont." She rose in a huff, slung her expensive purse over her shoulder, and marched to the door.

"You haven't heard the last from me. You're playing a dangerous game to come between me and what I want. And someone might get hurt."

"If you harbor any notion of marrying Max, and claiming my son..."

"That's not my intentions at all. Not at all, Ms. Bishop," she said calmly before flicking her long hair to the side and turning to face me. "We are having our own child, and as soon as the baby is born, we will send your son off to a private school. I will be traveling with Max, and I will not have time to raise another woman's child."

What a pair of balls! One quick thrust to the balls can send men to their knees, but this she-devil needs a stake through her heart and sunlight to bring her down. If she continues to fuck with me, she will get everything that's coming to her.

I flashed her a quick smile with no teeth.

I was stunned. It was a blow to me that I couldn't recover from soon. She shot me a fiendish smile with a mouth full of straight white teeth. The glare of her smile and the intent stayed long after she walked through the door. I blinked, and all I saw was a pair of dangerous black eyes and white teeth. I sank into the nearest chair. The room swirled around me as I sat thinking about what I had heard. It took some time for me to get my bearings, and when I did, I called Charles in a nervous huff.

"Can I see you today?"

"This is a wonderful surprise, Alex. What did I do to deserve this call?"

"You know what you did. You have been kind to me, and I need to express my feelings." *Maybe it is time to start dating.*

"I have a meeting this afternoon, but if you come to my office after work, I should be there at about seven o'clock. I'll have dinner prepared for you, and if I'm late, then you can eat and then sleep in one of the guest bedrooms."

"People will talk."

"Oh, Alex, let them. I don't run my life on what employees say or think, other than in business. My private life is mine and mine alone."

After a long day it was refreshing not to travel across town and then have to be bombarded by calls, and maybe a visit from Max.

I rang the bell to the penthouse suite. It was his office and home when he couldn't travel to his estate. A maid answered the door. Stepping into the dining room, I saw that the table was set with beautiful, monogrammed linen and crystal glassware. The chef placed the food in front of me as I sat gazing at Seattle's skyline. I lost myself in its beauty from seeing it so high in the air.

Charles called to say that he would be late. I ate, and when I finished, the maid cleared the table. I looked around and found a bedroom that suited my taste. The furnishings were sparse and European, with Monet's paintings hanging on the wall. The room I selected had a king bed. Sometime during the night, after catching up on work and reading a romance novel, I fell asleep. I felt a warm hand on my cheek, and I knew it was Charles. I didn't want to talk to him, so I pretended that I was dead to the world.

He leaned over and kissed my cheek. It was a caring and warm kiss. The kind a girl longed for from a man she loved. But I didn't love him, and I would have given everything to have that type of relationship with Max. Charles was as busy as Max, but he found time to be around when I needed him.

I hated myself for comparing the two men. I was now spending more time with Charles than I had been spending with Max. Max infuriated me so, because he left all my questions open. I still was yet to find out about the girl who by now had been buried. I never heard Max or Jonas say a word about her, but clearly one or both had had a relationship with her.

When I woke the next morning, there was a suit and accessories in front of my bed. I called out, and the maid came to tell me that Charles had an appointment and that he would see me tonight. *What does that mean, tonight? I said nothing about meeting him.*

After dressing for work, I tried to hide and take the elevator down to my office. I felt self-conscious, like a child who everyone knew had done something really bad, and everyone was pointing at me and whispering. I looked around, thinking I was safe when I entered the elevator, but then I heard someone say, "Good morning, Ms. Bishop."

My hand covering my mouth, I replied with a muffled, "Good morning," never turning to see who had discovered my secret. Who was I fooling? I put my head down and got off on my floor. I didn't know the person, but they knew me. I couldn't help but think about the conversation Charles and Jonas had when he was posing as Max, about having a mole in his company.

Happy not to have to drive to work, I sat at my desk and began reading about insurance and banking.

It was very early, and my smartphone rang. I decided to take Max's calls, because of Maxim. "Yes, Max. Is Maxim doing okay without me? Are you okay?" I hoped that was all this conversation would center on.

"Maxim is doing just great, but he misses his mother. I miss you too." I wanted to leap through the phone and kiss him and love him the way I knew I could.

"I'm working now, Max."

"Has Charles given you something that I couldn't? Does he kiss your...?"

"Oh my God. Stop it, Max. Charles and I haven't been intimate."

"Then why are you sleeping at his apartment?" He had gone the long way around to get to what he really wanted, and that was to discuss Charles St. John and me.

"How did you know that? Am I being followed?"

"I know everything you're doing." I craned my neck, looking around to see whether there were cameras on me or something that I hadn't noticed, and it occurred to me—the voice in the elevator. That voice was Max's spy.

"Max, this is not going to work."

"Can I see you?"

"For what?"

"I'm so jealous, Alex, I might do something crazy."

"Did you know that yesterday I had a visitor?" I didn't want to entertain his conversation and fall into his pity trap.

"Why? How would I know who visited you yesterday?" He didn't sound too convincing.

"You seem to know everything else," I countered. "Another one of your fiancées, this one was alive. A Jessica Beaumont paid a brief visit to my office." Max went silent. "Are you there, Max?"

"What did she say? I hope you didn't talk with her." I heard a break in Max's voice, as if they shared a secret.

"Yes, I did talk with her. She had plenty to say about your future with her and our son."

"There is no future with her. She is delusional."

"She appears to be very lucid, and she claims to know you quite well. Better than me. After all she said that she was raised with you and you two had been lovers since you were teens."

"What does that have to do with me now?"

"She is another one of your secrets you have concealed from me."

"I didn't think it was necessary to tell you about someone who doesn't exist in my life anymore."

"What did you do the night I left you at your fundraiser?"

"I took a flight out to New York. I dropped her home before then and I haven't seen her since. Please, believe me, Alex. I have nothing to do with her. I just want you. Come back to me, sweetheart?" My breath ceased, and I felt him caressing my body. I felt the warmth in his words sliding over my breasts as if it was his tongue.

"I can't," I said, taking hold of my senses.

"Then you leave me no choice, Alex." Max's voice alarmed me.

"What are you going to do, Max?"

"I'm going to ask the judge for permanent custody of Maxim," he said, as if he was about to take over a company and lay off the workers.

"You can't do that," I screamed.

"I can do anything I want, especially since I have evidence that you have been spending nights with St. John."

"Max, don't."

"Then, marry me."

I calmed myself, trying to think. Why should I accept his terms? I'd lived my life under my own terms even if I'd paid a price. It was my decision and my price to pay.

"You are not going to bully me any longer. I'm going to do everything in my power to stop you, Max."

"That sounds like a threat, Alex."

"Absolutely!" It was my bluff. I held one card, and it represented his heart. I was going to hold it until it became necessary to play it.

Chapter 9

Saturday marched in quietly and quickly. I prepared breakfast for myself and Crystal. We sat in silence, occasionally peeping at each other between sips of coffee. I didn't want to hear Crystal's problems, because I felt they were nothing compared to what I had been experiencing. But everyone would feel that their problems were worse than the next fellow's. I guessed the adage was true—you had to walk a mile in someone's shoes. So, I decided to let her get whatever was bothering her off her chest.

We had been staring at our scrambled eggs and picking at them with a fork, not eating. When I glanced up, Crystal's eyes were pooling with tears. "What's wrong today?" I asked, less sympathetic than I should have been.

"I don't know where Jonas is. I've been texting and texting him. I've even considered going around to his business."

"Oh no, don't do that." My voice rose quickly without a measure of control.

"But why?"

"Just calm down. He likes you..."

"He said he loved me," she said in a soft, childlike voice.

"Men always tell women they love them when they are horny and want to fuck, and they want to fuck all the time."

"Did Max tell you the same thing?" My brow knitted, and my eyes closed for a minute, tightening at the thought of what Max had said to me through the course of our relationship. I quickly hit the ball into Crystal's court.

"This is not about me, Crystal. Give him time. He's probably working for Max and couldn't call." I changed the subject immediately. "Hey, what about Joshua?" I asked, sounding positive and upbeat.

"I hear from him every day," Crystal said, sounding none too interested in discussing Josh.

"And you're not satisfied that he thinks enough of you to call every day? You want the bad boy—the one that can never be around when you really need him."

"It's the same with you, Alex." Crystal returned my serve. "St. John adores you, and you want Max. Look, Max and Jonas are twins. Do you think Max will be any different than Jonas? He took your son as he was telling you that he loved you." I stared at the pattern on the wall. I didn't know Crystal could be so deep.

Before I could defend Max, my phone rang. "Alex, this is Blake."

"I thought that I would never hear from you," I said, welcoming his call.

"You had my number. Why haven't you called?"

"I've had a few bad days, and I didn't want to burden you with my problems," I said, looking to replace Joshua as my friend and confidant.

"Can I meet you for lunch? I promise that you will not be disturbed by Blackstone. I have something important to tell you concerning the murder case of that heiress. I wanted to talk to you before the papers publish tomorrow."

"Yes. Yes, what time?" I was eager to learn about the newest developments in the case, and because Blake was willing to tell me something that wasn't common knowledge yet. He had been very tight-lipped on details. Maybe he thought that I would tell Max. I probably would have done that just to protect him.

"I'll pick you up at one o'clock. There's a rustic bar near the waterfront where cops hang out. They have great hamburgers and beer."

BLAKE DROVE UP IN A new Dodge truck. I waited outside and I climbed in, and he shut the door and entered. Hitting a button, he drove off. I smelled the newness of the truck, and it reminded me of the new Mercedes Max had given me. I had returned it because of my pride. Blake's radio was tuned into a country-and-western station, where a song was playing on the radio. I heard a lyric, "If you believe that I don't love you, then I can sell you a river in Arizona." My eyes swung around to Blake, but he kept his eyes on the road.

"Nice day, isn't it?" he said with a smile.

We made small talk about the weather, and exchanged observations on how we looked to each other. Whenever conversations started with the weather and ended with the weather, something was wrong.

"Are you going to tell me what was so important that you had to ask me to lunch?"

"I wanted to see you. I miss you and I like you." Blake placed his hand over mine as he drove. The electricity once reserved for Max seemed to register in my body. Not the overwhelming jolt I received whenever Max was near, but a calm energy that made me feel invigorated and full of life. Max had managed to sap the life out of me with his demands and his unyielding stance on Maxim.

"I explained to you that…" I stopped myself because I had forgotten there was no longer a "Max and I" to control how I felt. Now I needed stability and peace. Max had threatened to get full control of Maxim. I was disappointed and angry because Max had not touched me in months.

"I know about Mr. Blackstone, Alex. You explained about your loyalties and that you can't consider dating me because of him."

"It's not that anymore." Before I could continue the conversation, we arrived. It was an old, well-kept Irish bar with sawdust on the floors, which served drinks and food to the neighborhood men and women working on the docks.

"We're here."

We walked into a deserted bar with maybe three people seated at the long, weathered bar decorated with cigarette burns and bowls of peanuts and chips. Taking a booth in the back was my idea. I needed to talk to Blake without too much interference. Blake nodded his head as we passed. The bartender knew him; maybe Blake confided in him during his darkest moments. I wished I had someone to ease my burden.

Before we sat, Blake stood at the bar and ordered. "Two Heineken beers and two cheeseburgers, everything on it. He glanced at me for affirmation. I nodded. The bartender brought over two Heinekens.

"How did you know?"

"It's my job to know about people, especially friends. I asked you out to give you an update on the case involving that San Francisco heiress. Her family pushed the case, and tomorrow they are going to make an arrest. Because my partner is still on the case, he gave me this information, but he would not disclose who they were going to arrest. There are three people involved in this case."

I held my breath. My eyes darted around out of nervousness. I strummed the table. Blake's eyes followed my movements. I didn't want to hear the names. Even though I had vowed to never talk to Max, I loved him dearly and I would do anything for it not to be him. I grabbed Blake's arm in anticipation of the names.

"Jonas's name was not on the radar until I discovered that Max had a twin brother," Blake stated, looking in my eyes and searching for something. "Their DNA is the same, so we had to add him to the list. As you well know, Max is at the top of the list, but now we have a new twist. Jessica Beaumont is one of the suspects."

"But how...?"

"We think Jessica may have helped Maximilian cover up the crime, or she framed him, but we can't prove it now. Jonas had been dating the heiress under Max's name. That's why the report in the papers cited Max as her fiancée."

"So, Max was not lying about not having anything to do with the heiress."

"It appears to be the case. But until we narrow it down to one of two people, his name will still be linked to the dead girl."

The barkeeper brought over the cheeseburgers. I stared at mine but couldn't eat. I knew that I would be hungry soon after I got over the shock of hearing about Max. I had no doubt that that she-devil Jessica Beaumont had something to do with the heiress's death by the warning she had given me about Max, but that wouldn't hold up in court. It would be my word against hers.

"I had a visitor yesterday. Jessica came to my job and threatened me."

"She did what? Be careful, because she is our number-one suspect. I'm going to make sure no harm comes to you. I will stake out your house and job if it's okay with you."

"Yeah. Sure." I would have agreed to anything to discover the truth about Max and bring an end to this and get on with my life.

Blake took me home, and later that night I peered through the window and saw his truck parked across the street in the dark. I felt safe. My thoughts strayed. *Where is Max when I need him?* My phone rang.

"Hello, Charles."

"Sunday would be a great time to teach you how to ride. Can I send a car for you tomorrow morning?" My mind drifted to Blake. I figured that he would have to go home sometime, and then I would visit Charles. Deep down, I felt as if I was cheating on Max and Blake with Charles, but in reality, it was only Max.

"Sunday would be fine, but you have to promise me that you won't keep me past two o'clock. I have to take care of some things before work on Monday."

"I promise."

Sunday rolled around, and there were no calls from Max. I became concerned and tried to keep myself from calling him. I wanted to enjoy my time with Charles without thinking about anything or anyone. However, the thought of him or maybe Jonas being arrested was devastating. I knew Max could escape whatever happened to him, because of his lawyers, but Jonas was different. He had been on drugs, and he was into all manner of sexual deviancy. I had completely forgotten about Crystal. I hadn't seen her in a few days. I thought she was with Jonas.

Looking outside for Blake's truck, I noticed that it was not in the usual spot. And prompt as usual was Charles's limo, pulling up to my house at 7:30 a.m. on the dot. I hurried into the car and picked up the local newspaper even though the *New York Times* and the *Washington Post* lay nearby. On the front page, in bold headlines that sucked the air from my lungs, was a picture of Max. I looked further and it said: **Jonas Blackstone Arrested in Seattle for the Salacious Necktie Murder of San Francisco's Real-Estate Heiress.**

My phone began ringing. First it was Crystal. I didn't know what to tell her. Then it was Max. I had to take his call.

"Alex, baby." He sounded as if he was dying. His voice was hoarse and weak. After all, he had been through a lot in a few days. I could hear defeat in that voice. He loved his brother.

"I know. It's you. I'm sorry, Max. What can I do?"

"I need you. I need to see you. I'm in San Francisco trying to arrange bail for Jonas. I don't think it will happen. The police have too much on him, and he confessed."

"Why would he confess?"

"He thought it was me. He wanted to help me out. I didn't do it, and Jonas didn't murder that girl."

"I don't understand. Who could have done such a thing?"

"Any number of people. Please, let me come to you. I don't want to be alone."

"Max, I'll meet you at your hotel. I need some privacy away from Crystal. She is frantic now. I can't face her."

"I'll be there about nine tonight. I'll call ahead and send a car for you at seven. I'll tell them to expect my wife. That will get you into my penthouse without any problems."

I had to tell the driver to turn around and take me home. I called Charles and gave an excuse—a small lie I could live with. The truth would have been too painful.

***

MAX'S CAR ARRIVED AT seven. I was happy to get away from all the crazy stuff going on with Jonas and now with Crystal and Josh. I arrived at Max's hotel. The driver helped me out of the car and whispered to the doorman, and he greeted me with a wide smile, escorting me into the lobby. I had never been to this hotel. It had his brand on it, with its ultramodern stainless-steel and glass furniture, and light fixtures out of a science-fiction movie.

I took a deep breath; I had to see Max to give him a feeling of comfort and to reassure him that he was not alone. I knew how he felt from being all alone and living where I could after running away from home. I had no family to confide in and to give me peace of mind. I wanted to let Max know that I was his family.

I reached his penthouse and walked into the large room. It resembled most of his hotel suites, with large foyers leading to the living area and then several bedrooms and baths, but this one had a full-service kitchen. There were killer views from the panoramic windows. This view overlooked the Needle and the harbor.

I sat on the large sofa, taking in the view. *I could get used to this,* I thought. Was I doing the very thing I had accused Josh of doing—selling out? Since I'd fallen into Max's world, I hadn't been able to escape, so the best thing I could do was to embrace it. When in Rome, as they would say.

Throwing my shoes to the side, I padded into the rest of the penthouse, looking around. I found the kitchen and opened the fridge—nothing but water and champagne. I decided to embrace the luxuries surrounding me. Tired of cooking a fast meal to save money, I was ready for room service.

I ordered lobster for two, caviar just to try it, and an assortment of desserts—and why not open a bottle of champagne Max had in the wine fridge? When I had completed ordering the obscenely high-priced meal that I would not have to pay for, I heard the elevator door open.

My heart fluttered, and in walked my Mr. Black with a bag of groceries in one hand and with the other he held on to a black satchel. He then threw it to the floor.

"I ordered supper."

"But I was going to cook for you." He looked like a child that had been disappointed after careful choosing an imitation pearl necklace for his mother, and then finding out that she already had one, and that one was real.

"Max, I can't believe you would do this for me. You look tired."

"I am, but I would do anything for you."

My thoughts trailed, and I thought that this was not the time to bring up Maxim.

He walked to the kitchen and deposited the bag on the counter, then he returned with a smile of relief. "Okay." His eyes brightened and he took off his coat and threw it on the chair near the couch. He wore a gray suit, which was a surprising change. Standing in the same spot, he pulled the tie from his white shirt and let it drop. Then he smiled and opened his shirt. With his finger pointing in my direction, he mouthed, "Come here."

I looked around, and then I said, "Who me?"

He nodded and said, "Yes, you."

I walked slowly until I reached him. His hungry mouth found mine, and our tongues embraced in a wild flurry of passion. The grunts and moans were something you would hear on Animal Planet. We were engaging in heated foreplay. Max shoved his tongue in and out as if it was an extension of his penis and my mouth was my vagina. I sucked his tongue firmly as I would his hard, aroused penis. Saliva escaped from the side of our mouths like his semen draining from a quick orgasm.

His kisses clouded my memory.

I forgot what tore me from him. I forgot what made me leave him. I forgot why I had come to be with him at this moment. All I wanted was to be is in his arms, to be taken and plunged into an orgy of vile, unending sex, with the pain and satisfaction that came from being well-fucked.

I pulled his jacket off and then unbuckled his belt. Looking at me in surprise, Max unzipped his pants and said, "Go to your knees." Before I had time to think about anything or anyone, Max had his hard, erect penis in one hand, holding it to my face, and with the other he slid his thumb around my lips, circling the ridges of my mouth as he had done on my anus. He placed his penis in my mouth, and my dream of him standing over me with his hard dick rammed in my mouth had come true.

I glanced at him. His eyes were closed, and he mumbled, "Oh, Alex, you don't know how long I have wanted this from you." He pushed and pulled and held a handful of my hair in his fist as he directed my head to the movement of his body.

"Alex, I'm coming. Don't let me come now. It's too soon. You are making me too weak for you."

Not weak enough. But just you wait, and you won't deny me anything, I thought. Just as he requested, I pulled away from sucking him hard, and slowly and gradually I took my mouth away from his hard, wonderful penis until his body calmed, and drips of come subsided, and he had control once more. *This is my present to you. Allowing you to think you have control, my horny, beautiful fuck.*

Standing and locking eyes with Max, I walked backward and sat down on the sofa, then as Max looked at me, I took off my blouse and bra. I held my nipples between my fingers, teasing him. Then I eased out of my skirt and pantyhose. I sat naked and opened my legs, fingering my bud. "Now it's your turn. I want you on your knees, and I want you to eat me for as long as I command you to."

Max's eyes glistened. "It's not how long I can eat you, but how long you can take me eating that beautiful cunt of yours."

I was more than ready. The night held infinite possibilities, and I wanted to explore all of them before dawn.

He crouched between my legs, and his tongue glided over his top lip. He pushed his head into my opening and pulled me forward, placing my legs on his shoulders. Planting his head between my legs and surveying my bud with his tongue gave him extreme pleasure. I could hear the sound of his quick heartbeat, and he had the look of a man who had found what he wanted in life. Lifting his head, he locked eyes with me. "I could spend my nights and days eating your pussy. When are you going to commit to me?" He didn't wait for an answer; he went back to the thing he liked best, bringing me joy and satisfying his slavish erotic desire for oral sex.

"Max, I am having an orgasm. I'm not like you; I have to do it now."

"Please, sweetheart, wait for me. My dick needs you. I need to look in your face when you come. I don't know when I will see you again."

So he's like a hibernating bear stocking up for winter.

Chapter 10

Max and I lay side by side on the floor after round one of a marathon of sex. The bell rang, and I realized I had forgotten that I had ordered dinner. He scrambled to put on his pants. I got up to run and he threw me his coat. "What will the waiter think?"

"I don't care. Maybe he'll think that Mr. Blackstone is getting a piece from his hot wife. Maybe he'll tell the others that I'm not homosexual."

"Well, are you?"

He turned with his bright, expensive smile and his dimples carving dents in both sides of his jaw and said, "I'll let you answer that." He opened the door and told the waiter to place everything on the floor, because he was having a picnic with his new wife.

The waiter never looked in my direction, setting the food down on a white tablecloth he had spread on the floor. Like a dutiful employee, he smiled and backed out of the room. "They probably think we're crazy. That's what they think of the rich," he said, opening a bottle of wine. Max had forgotten that I was included in that group who thought that the rich were arrogant, insane, unsympathetic people.

As Max prepared to pour me a drink to celebrate our compromise, a phone rang. By the old-fashioned ring it was my phone. I had left it on just in case there was news from Jonas and Maxim. I had to be available out of my concern for Jonas and my child. Max stood, searching around the room for my phone, and found it. He looked at it.

"You have a missed call from Charles St. John." His forehead wrinkled with disapproval, his eyes seething with jealousy and his thick eyebrows narrowing. "Did you fuck him, Alex?"

"Would you believe me if I told you?" Max didn't say a word, and turned his back and tilted his head to the right.

"Then why would I waste my time to go through that with you?" The conversation had taken an ugly turn. After the wonderful lovemaking we were back to where we started.

I stood, and the only cover I had on my naked body dropped to the floor. His eyes wandered to my mound, and he grabbed my hand. "You are not going anywhere."

"And who is going to stop me?"

"I am," Max said, throwing me across his knee. He began paddling my ass with his large hands.

"Stop, Max. You are hurting me."

"Yes. But it's making me feel a lot better." He stopped, and his hand slid over my butt, and he gently began rubbing where he had turned my butt cheeks red. "This makes me want you more. I don't know what is wrong with me." He reached for the soft butter on a tray and rubbed it on me. He then circled the rim of my anus and slid his buttered fingered into my opening, while with the finger of his right hand he played with my folds. He then placed his finger into my vagina.

With one finger in my ass and the other on my clit, I managed to get to my knees, propping my body against the couch. Max took out the finger in my anus and guided his hard dick into my opening and plunged forward. I felt it in my stomach, and then it hit a wall and would go no farther. His movements were hard and powerful, and when I thought I would burst, he slowed down and used his large finger in my vagina to simulate a dick. I was being fucked at both holes, and Max's movements were so in sync that a chill raced up my spine and settled at the nape of my neck.

"I'm coming, Max."

"Go ahead and come, baby. I'm going to be here a while. I want to make love to you so anyone that comes after me knows that I have been here."

"No one has ever made love to me but you, Max."

"Please, say that again." His movements became wild and erratic. He pushed into me harder than he had ever.

"No one has ever fucked me, Max. Only you." His head fell back, and my head rested on his chest as he continued his drilling into my anus. His heart beat quickly, and he exhaled and grabbed my hips with both hands and brought me into him. Then he let out a cry of satisfaction, and I felt his come and his dick ease from my body.

The invasion of that part of my body had lasted long enough that a part of me had disappeared, but I found what was left of me, which was exciting and sexual. The intensity of the lovemaking was like exorcising an alien entity; I was exhausted, breathless, and weak. Max picked me up in his large arms and brought me to the shower.

"Are you okay?"

"I'm doing fine."

He washed my body with such care. I was seeing a different man. I saw a man who could change. I saw a man who showed his feelings. I saw a man who cared, but whether he would change or not, I would have to take a chance on him. After our shower, we ate. Max laid me down in his bed and climbed in with me. We lay entwined in each other's arms, asleep. Max slept that night. I think he had not slept since Jonas was arrested.

I woke, and Max wasn't lying in the bed. All my fears began to revisit me. I had fallen for the lie after I had convinced myself that he had changed. The only one that had changed was me. I searched around for the damn notes that he was notorious for, but I couldn't find one. Then I smelled coffee and eggs and bacon. I looked up, and standing in the doorway was Max with a tray.

Sitting up, I rubbed my eyes and passed my hand over my hair. I must have looked a sight. I had been sleeping hard; rubbing my hand across my mouth, I felt a piece of my hair and the indention it had made in my cheek.

"You are so beautiful," Max said, looking at me as if I were a painting by Monet hanging on his wall. I guessed when a woman felt loved, she was beautiful, but that was hardly how I felt. I was hungry, and my breasts and feet were swollen like a Botero sculpture.

"Can you believe that the first job I had was working in my foster parents' restaurants? I started as a bus boy and made my way up to a waiter. Every summer during my college years I could count on that job. I was good at it. I learned about the restaurant and hotel business."

He placed the tray across my lap. "Good morning, sleepyhead." Then he leaned forward and kissed me on my cheek.

"Max, you didn't have to do this." I sat straight up, and before my words could drop, I had a piece of toast dangling from my mouth.

"I know, but I wanted to. I want you to see that we can have a good life together and I will take care of you. If you marry me, I'm going to sell some of my business ventures." I looked up with raised eyebrows. "Especially the hotels in Las Vegas," he said. "We can raise our son together. Go to Little League, soccer, or football games. Do something besides roam the world looking to build more hotels and never enjoying the money I've made. I want to take you to Paris. It's not fun if I can't give you something. What's the purpose?"

I realized how unhappy Max had been. I wanted to make him happy, but I needed answers that he refused to give me. Max sat on the bed. I fixed my tea and took a sip. "Max, what are you going to do about Jonas?"

"Until the truth is uncovered, there isn't much I can do. He can't do time; he's mentally unstable. Now he's worried about Crystal leaving him for Joshua."

"Max, I know you love your brother, but don't do anything to Joshua to cause him any problems. I know Joshua. He will bounce back from Crystal, and Crystal likes Jonas a lot."

"I wouldn't do anything. I have enough problems with you." We glanced at each other, and he took my hair and placed it behind my ear.

I looked casually at the clock on the wall, and then I screamed.

"What day is it? I was supposed to be at work this morning. I will lose my job."

"You don't need a job. I called St. John and told him that you will no longer work for him."

"Why would you do that, Max?"

"I thought that because we were finally intimate, everything was better between us."

"You don't know women. You must have thought that you could fuck that Beaumont woman and say it was over between the two of you and that was that. Well it wasn't. And what you did by calling Charles is unforgivable. Where is my phone?"

"Alex, if you call St. John and don't marry me now, then it's over."

Did he just say that? Am I supposed to beg him not to leave me? Just like that after he has fucked me all night? I can't believe what I'm hearing. If it's not his way, it's the highway? Weren't those supposed to be my words? Clearly someone has gotten full of himself. He wasn't acting that way until I told him I have never had another man and will never have another man but him. That's what I get for confessing.

I grimaced at Max and retrieved my smartphone. Max stood watching me as I hit a button, and then Charles came on the line.

"Charles." I glanced at Max, standing and waiting, daring me to continue. "I want you to disregard what Max said. I'm not quitting my job, and I am not marrying Max."

Max was silent, and his eyes were glazed over as if he couldn't see me. He walked out of the room, into the next. I placed the tray on the table with the breakfast Max had cooked for me. I tried to get up, but I was too weak.

Oh, how I wished it was yesterday and I could go back.

I pulled the covers up to my chest and closed my eyes. I heard Max talking, and somehow I fell back to sleep. When I woke, I felt someone staring down at me. "I'm leaving now, Alex. Stay as long as you want. Hell, I'll give you this apartment."

"I don't want anything from you but my son."

"He comes with the father. Take it or leave it."

"That's your compromise?"

"I don't compromise."

"That's a threat," I said.

"Absolutely!" And Max walked away from me leaving me in his bed. I scrambled to get to my feet. I wasn't going to let him have the last word, but I was too late; he had gone. Where? I didn't know. I never knew.

Would I know where he was if I were his wife?

I DREADED RETURNING to my bungalow because I had to face Crystal and her questions. I walked in the door and found Crystal sitting facing the television but not watching it. Her cheeks were red, and her eyes swollen.

"Where have you been, Alex? I called everywhere looking for you. I saw St. John yesterday at his restaurant, and he asked about you. No one could find you."

"I was with Max."

"You said..."

"I know what I said. It's been a long day." I threw my things down in the dining area and lumbered to my room. Crystal followed me into the room, waiting for answers. I started to undress, and when she could no longer wait for me to respond to her, she questioned me.

"What is happening to Jonas? Did Blackstone get him out of jail?"

"I don't think Jonas can get bond because he's a flight risk." She put her head in her hand and sank into a chair near my bed. "Max has too much money, and the judge knows he would do anything for his brother."

"I need him out of jail," Crystal said, flailing her arms.

"I'm sure he doesn't want to be there, Crystal. You need to calm down and have some patience." Here I was, giving advice to her when I never took anyone's advice.

"Do you think he could have done such a thing to that woman, Alex? Not Jonas, I mean Max," Crystal stated. I grimaced. "He has a dark nature," Crystal said, trying to convince me of Max's guilt.

"No. No, neither one is capable of doing that, Crystal. Max will take care of everything."

"If he did it, he might want to frame Jonas."

"Stop it, Crystal. Nothing is going to happen to Jonas, and blaming Max is not helping the situation." I climbed into my bed, and Crystal stayed curled up in the chair looking for reassurance, which was a waste of time, because I needed some myself.

Chapter 11

I showed up to work the following day feeling exhausted and out of it. I shouldn't have even been there, but I didn't want Charles to feel as if I was taking advantage. I was aware that I wasn't doing the work I had being paid for, and by the stares, whispers, and looks on everyone's faces on my floor, they felt the same way I did. However, I was determined to make this work without Charles's intervention.

"Good morning, Ms. Bishop," one of the eager interns said. By the smirk plastered on his face, he was used to kissing ass and knowing secrets. His eyes and raised eyebrows said it all—*you can't fool me; you got your job by fucking the big boss, and you will be moving up soon, and I will have your job.* As he passed, nodding in my direction, I received a call.

The voice was professional and warm. "Ms. Bishop, can you come to my office at this time?" It didn't have the salacious sound of Max when he first hired me in San Francisco, but the tone had the same intent.

"Yes, sir. I'll be there in a minute." I didn't know what I would find, but I hoped it wasn't a naked Charles St. John, because I would have to quit on the spot. *How could I think such a thing? Charles has been more than a gentleman.*

I dashed to the elevator, and in seconds, I was at the top floor. I rang the bell, and when the door opened, Charles stood there in a pair of gray slacks and a white V-neck silk sweater. He looked deliciously handsome. "Come in, Alex." I walked into the room and stood with panic on my face. I just knew he was going to fire me, but wouldn't he let someone else do that?

"I have good news for you." My breath eased out. "The judge in family court agreed to hear your case, and my lawyers are preparing to argue before him. I know a few judges myself. If everything goes well, you will have your son back within a week."

I ran to Charles and looped my arms around his neck. Looking into his cool blue eyes, I leaned into his lips and his mouth met mine. My head began to swirl as if I was on a merry-go-round. I felt dizzy, I felt happy, I felt faint, and I felt his kiss and his evasive tongue. It did something to me. I had to admit I liked it. Pulling myself away from him before I would regret the next step, which was climbing into his bed, I said, "Thank you."

All of a sudden the hold that Max had over me did not appear to be as strong. I could see, think, and feel again. Charles was a handsome man. His blue eyes and slanted smile seduced me in a way Max had not. His easy manner was the opposite of Max's direct stand-your-ground attitude. But I wasn't ready to give up on Max, and I wasn't ready to be unfaithful to a man I had wanted from the moment I laid eyes on him.

"Alex, have a seat." I found a chair facing the window looking out into the city. I tried to read Charles's magnificent face, which concealed his feelings. He hesitated, and then said, "Would you marry me?"

My mouth opened wide, and I didn't know what to say. I didn't say no, and I wouldn't dare say yes, but I said, "Wow. You know how to sweep a girl off her feet. Me, why me? Why do you want to marry me?"

"I want to take care of you. I want to take care of you and your son," he said, cupping my chin with a soft touch of his hand.

"You know very well that Max will never stand for…"

"For me marrying you?" he queried.

"No, that's not exactly what I wanted to say. He will not stand for another man raising his son."

"So, you are not going to marry Max, and you can't marry anyone else because of him." I hadn't thought of it that way. Charles had me pondering my future. I was too young to think about that. But now I had to. "I can give you the things you need to prevent Max from taking your son from you again. He can cite the bungalow as an unsuitable home for his child. And you are unable to pay for a private school."

"But once I have him in my custody, he will have to pay child support and I can afford better living conditions and a school." I thought my argument was convincing, at least to me.

Charles went to his knees in front of me, meeting my eyes, placing his hands on mine. "Max can claim that he would be a better parent because you are not married, and you never told him about his child. There are so many things that he may say, true or false. Furthermore, there is the issue of someone kidnapping his son."

Confused and bewildered, my face lifted upward, my eyes closed, and my head dropped back. Charles had thrown every reason in the world at me why I should marry him.

"What do you say, Alex? Will you?" I held my breath. He saw me hesitate and my eyes search the room for an answer. He added, "I promise you that if you don't think we are compatible, you can get an annulment. I will pay you enough money that you won't have to worry about Maximilian Blackstone unless you want to. I will you do one better. I will let you have access to my lawyers for an annulment or divorce if it doesn't work out and I will put everything in writing."

"Give me time to think about this. It's too much," I said, shaking my head.

"I'm taking the day off. Take a ride with me to the beach."

"I don't know if I can." He grabbed my hands and pulled me to my feet.

"My car is downstairs, and I feel as if I'm twenty again." His smile lit up my heart and made me feel safe and secure. I agreed. We took an elevator reserved for Charles. I was happy to sneak past all the people looking to gossip about me, especially the mole Max had planted in Charles's bank.

He placed his hand behind my waist and led me through the doors. When I stepped out, there was an expensive silver sports car waiting with an attendant opening the door. Charles opened my door, and someone rushed up and took our picture. "That's what happens when I drive instead of taking my limo." I thought nothing of it and sat and swiveled my legs around, planting then in the car on its lush floor mats. He walked around and sat behind the wheel.

Looking to him, I asked, "What kind of car is this?"

"A Maserati Quattro Porte."

"Oh. Okay." I giggled a little. It must have been the nervous laugh that gave me away. Glancing my way with a smile, Charles knew I had never seen one before.

"Max is a collector. Why hasn't he taken you for a ride in it?" he queried.

"He's been busy, and we have had a contentious relationship. Can we talk about something else?" I shook my head, closing my eyes.

"Whatever you wish. You haven't had lunch."

"I want a big, juicy cheeseburger," I said with the eagerness of a teenager.

"Me too," he said with a wide smile. I couldn't imagine Charles driving up in that car to a fast-food window and ordering a hamburger. I thought he was trying to show me that he was human and just a man, which was more than I could say about Max. In some ways I was in awe of Max. He had control of his feelings. Maybe that was why I tried so hard to force emotions from him with my constant denial of him.

I might have been secretly afraid of losing him, because I would go so far with him and then give in. I never wanted to lose that man. I never wanted him out of my life, and I never wanted him not to pay attention to me. But Charles was forcing me to examine my life and what I wanted from it.

CHARLES DROPPED ME at home at the end of the day. And as soon as I walked into the house, placed my purse on a table, and kicked off my shoes, I drifted into the kitchen to get a bottle of water, but I heard a knock at the door. "Who the hell is it this time?" I grumbled. The knock was loud; I knew that knock. It was the big, bad wolf. All of me said *don't open it*, but I did. Max burst through the open door.

"Do you understand, Max, I'm not the only person that lives here?" I said, standing near the doorframe. "What are you doing here? Please, leave."

"What is wrong with you, Alex? What is going on with you? I leave you for a moment and you are fucking St. John."

"Leave, Max. We have been through this a thousand times. I don't think we have any more to say to each other." Max turned on his heel, not expecting me to send him on his way, and then he swung around. He had more to say, and I was not going to dismiss him.

"I can't leave. What is it you want from me? I have my son and Jonas to deal with, and every minute I am worrying about you."

"I'm not your concern. Our child is. I'm not your child. I'm a woman. Not that girl you screw when you can't sleep. I have my wants and desires. I have a life away from you." Max walked in my direction, and I backed up, moving away from him. "You have no excuse for what you have done to us, Max." I saw a crack in his armor. His eyes telegraphed his concern, and sadness blanketed them. "You have taken my child from me. I knew you were a lot of things, but I never knew you would be ruthless and cold with me."

"I'm trying to change, Alex. It's not enough that I love you and want you with me and our son?" he questioned.

"No it's not enough. I have to be able to make my own decisions and not have you manipulate a situation to gain control of me."

Max acted as if I had been talking to the wall. His eyes wandered around the room and settled on my lips and then my breasts.

"Are you fucking him? Tell me, Alex." He came close to me with fiery eyes.

"Did you fuck that Beaumont woman?" I said to counter.

His eyes calmed.

"That was a long time ago. She's acting as if it was just yesterday. I'm handling the matter."

I've heard that before. I closed my eyes and shook my head. Max understood my body language.

"Max, Charles asked me to marry him, and I'm considering it."

"He's using you to hurt me. He knows that I'm weighed down with Jonas, and now he realizes that Jonas was part of the strategy to take business from him. He wants you and my son. He's trying to destroy me."

I looked at Max in disbelief. "You are creating something that doesn't exist. What are you talking about?"

"His dead wife, she is the mirror image of you when she was your age. She died without having children for him, and he's trying to replace her with you and my son. Can't you see that?" He held my wrist. I pulled away from him. "He's not genuine. He wants to make you into the image of his dead wife."

I stepped back. "That is ridiculous," I said, raising my voice higher than normal. "I can't see anything other than you wanting to disrupt my life, and I don't want to deal with you now."

Max turned and walked away. I couldn't read his expression. My heart pounded out of control, and I had to brace myself on the doorframe. I was afraid—afraid that he would never come back. I closed the door behind me, and when I looked through the window I saw Max leaving and Blake driving up and parking.

Waiting at the door until Blake walked to the porch, I was out of breath. He rushed up the steps. "Are you all right, Alex? I saw Max through your window, but I couldn't get here in time."

"It was nothing, Blake. Max wouldn't hurt me."

"What's wrong, Alex?"

"I don't know what to do. I'm caught between two billionaires." Blake brought me into his arms and held me for a few. "Do you want some coffee?" Blake nodded yes, and I asked him in.

Crystal appeared in the doorway to her room. "I didn't know you were here, Crystal."

"I just talked to Jonas, and he's having a terrible time in jail. He can't stand the confinement. And Max hasn't been there to see him. Please, ask Max to do something." I held Crystal until she felt better. She disappeared into her room and closed the door. I glanced at Blake.

He watched as I prepared the coffeemaker. It only brewed one cup at a time. I brought it to him, and he sat quietly looking down into the cup. "Can you do something to help, Blake? Do you think Jonas killed that girl?"

"I can't discuss the case, and no I don't think he did it."

Please, don't say Max killed her. I couldn't handle it, I thought.

"All I can tell you is that it will all be over soon, Alex."

As I left to get my coffee, my smartphone sitting on the dining table rang.

"Hello, Alex?"

"Yes, speaking."

"Don't you recognize my voice? It's Josh."

"Oh my God, Josh. Where are you?"

"I'm in Seattle. I flew in last night."

"Josh, I've missed you so much." I almost forgot about Blake until he stood and waved at me and gestured for me to continue talking on the phone. He mouthed that he would keep in touch. I blew him a kiss and he caught it and put it next to his heart. Blake let himself out and got into his Dodge truck and left as Josh rambled on about how he missed me and Crystal.

"How about if I drive over and take my favorite girls out to dinner?"

"I don't know if that's a good idea. Crystal has been going through something lately."

"She's not pregnant, is she?"

"Why would that cross your mind?"

"I wouldn't mind being a father."

"Oh, please, Josh, let's not talk about that now."

"When? Where is Crystal and why hasn't she answered my calls?" A long silence came between us.

"I'll see you tonight at your apartment," I said, hurrying him off the phone.

"Make sure you bring Crystal here, because there is something I need to tell her."

"She has a job, you know. I can't guarantee anything."

We said goodbye and I knocked on Crystal's door. "Come in."

Crystal lay draped across her bed. The room was a mess—dirty clothes thrown across chairs and on the floor surrounding the bed, day-old Chinese takeout, and drinks on trays had the room smelling like a dead rat.

"How can you sleep in here like that?"

"I'm depressed."

"Have you gone to work?"

"No, I called in sick for a few days."

"You have to get yourself together, because Josh is here."

"Here?" Her eyes widened and she stuck her head under the covers. "Tell him to go away."

"He's not here; he's at his apartment in Seattle."

"Good. I can't see him now. I can't see anyone. I miss Jonas and he needs me. Josh doesn't need me. I love Jonas." I couldn't believe that Crystal would fall for a misfit like Jonas. But then, looking at the guys she had dated, Jonas and Joshua were the best of the bunch, and Joshua was far better than anything she had found.

After Crystal cried and convinced me that Josh was better off without her, I was sold on the idea. But she left me to break the news to Josh.

Excited to see my friend, I dressed and drove to Max's hotel, where Josh had an apartment on the thirty-third floor. I dropped my VW off with the valet. He took my keys as if I had the plague. That drew a silent laugh from me.

The doorman opened the door wide and gave me a glance of recognition. When I had walked halfway through the lobby, I heard the doorman say, "Welcome back, Mr. Blackstone and Ms. Beaumont." I turned in time to see them enter, him smiling and her hand looped under his and his left hand placed over hers.

I paused a moment because he hadn't reached his private elevators. I wanted him to see me so there could be no denying that he was with her or the standard excuse. Jonas was in county jail, but the look on Max's face said that he didn't give a damn. He was going to get whatever Jessica Beaumont specialized in, which from looking at her could be any number of things.

When Max and Jessica reached the elevators, he had to cross my path to get to his penthouse elevator. As he made a right, I crossed in front of him to my left. I turned and faced him. "I hope she makes you happy," I said with trembling lips.

I thought my heart had stopped beating and that I had died. The opening of the elevator doors sent a whoosh of air, and I knew I was alive, at least for the moment.

Max startled and his eyes opened wide, not expecting to see me. And I was so upset that I couldn't see or think. He stopped, pulling away from Jessica to go after me, but she wouldn't let go of his arm. All he could do was call my name. "Alex. Alex." I ran into the elevator, and the door closed behind me.

My hand never stopped ringing Josh's bell. I needed someplace to run and hide. I wanted to forget what I had seen, but there were too many visuals to process. I couldn't buy a smile from Max, but he was giving it away to that bitch.

"Whoa. What's going on, Alex?" When Josh opened the door I grabbed him and threw myself into his arms.

"I love you too, Alex."

"Oh Josh, I just saw Max with Jessica Beaumont." Josh raised an eyebrow. "The one he took to the fundraiser." He shook his head acknowledging who I referred to. I dropped onto his couch. Josh rushed to open a bottle of wine. He poured me a glass.

"Here. Take this." I reached for the glass and swallowed a large gulp.

The wine began working. It was doing what I hoped it would—make me drunk. I confessed all my sins. I told Josh about Charles and Max. I told him how Max had been pressuring me to marry him, and that if I didn't he would never let me have my son. I told Josh about the marriage proposal from Charles, and that I was considering his proposal, at which point Joshua stared at me and then blinked and sighed.

"I can't believe that you would even consider marrying St. John. You are half his age, and he is still mourning his dead wife. Whenever I've been in his presence, he pulls out a picture of her and shows it all around. And he tells everyone that she was the most beautiful woman he has ever met. Do you want to marry a man like that?"

"Now you sound like Max. Are you now over in public relations, or are you a goodwill ambassador for Blackstone?"

"I'm just stating the facts, Alex." I squirmed in my seat and polished off another glass of wine. "I saw her picture, Alex. He showed it to Max too, and she looks exactly like you. Only you are a younger version. So, maybe Max has something there when he says that he is trying to re-create a version of his wife."

"That's just not true. And there are a lot of people that resemble one another," I said.

"Do what you want, but I think you're making a bad choice. I would take a man who wanted me for myself instead of one who would try to remake me after someone else. That's just creepy."

"I can live with creepy; I just can't live with someone dominating me."

"Then you dominate him. Isn't that what you do? Aren't those the games you and Max played?" I gave Josh the finger.

"Josh, I'm serious."

"That's your problem. You are too serious. I tell you what; let's go to the bar downstairs and listen to jazz. There's this great piano player. We can get drunk, and you can tell me about Crystal."

I wished Josh would get drunk enough that I could tell him about Jonas and Crystal. I agreed, because I didn't want to be confined in a room with Josh and have to think about what Max was doing with Jessica.

We headed downstairs. Getting off the elevator, we slid to the right and into a cozy room where soft music was playing. We sat at a booth and ordered Scotch and water for Josh and a glass of red wine for me. We could see into the lobby because of the glass façade, and when the waiter placed the bottle of wine on the table, I looked up and saw Max and Jessica, all smiles, heading for the door. He had his limo waiting for them. He even opened the door for her.

That should be me, I thought.

I nudged Josh, and he looked up and glanced at the two. "They look pretty cozy, Alex. Are you sure you want to let her have him? You were made for each other. You look good together. You understand each other, and your sex habits are compatible."

By that time I was drunk. "What do you know about my sexual habits?"

Joshua snapped his fingers. "Remember me? I'm the guy that went through all this shit with you."

"Oh yeah, my friend Josh." I looped my arm around his neck. "Josh, you are too good for Crystal."

"What do you mean? You haven't said a word about her all night."

"There is something you need to know," I said, not realizing that I should let Crystal break the news herself.

"Let me speak, Alex." Josh put his finger up to stop me from rambling on. "I need you to tell Crystal that I have found someone else, and that I didn't mean to hurt her."

My eyes widened. "Did I hear you correctly?"

"Yes, and I need you to tell her. I don't want to see her cry."

"Trust me, there won't be any tears, and I will be happy to break the news to her."

Josh kissed my cheek, and we kept on with the business of getting drunk. We had to hold each other up as we climbed into the elevator taking us to Josh's room. I explained all the things that had happened since he had been in Hong Kong. I talked about Jonas's arrest, and Josh didn't seem surprised.

I couldn't bring myself to tell him about Crystal and Jonas. He was happy now that he thought he had broken a woman's heart, and to tell him that Crystal had fucked Jonas before Josh set down in Hong Kong would have burst his last balloon and taken away his stud credit.

⸻ ◈ ⸻

WE WOKE THE NEXT MORNING with headaches. I lay across Joshua's bed, and he sprawled on the floor wrapped in a blanket his grandmother had given him. The sun peeking in through the sheer curtains woke me; otherwise, I would have been in a sleepy, drunken daze. I walked to the bathroom, stepping over Josh, careful not to wake him. After a long flight, he needed to sleep, even if it was on the floor.

Rummaging through his closet, I found a flannel shirt and pajama pants. I took them to change into after my shower. Turning on the shower, I stood there letting the water bathe me and wash the scent of alcohol from all my pores. Stepping out, I pulled up the pajama pants and put on the shirt. I threw my dress into a bag and padded into the kitchen for coffee and some sort of bread.

After putting on the coffee, I walked to the door to get the paper. I wondered what kind of news would be printed about Jonas. After reaching down and taking the paper, I opened it to the front page. I felt stunned, confused, and crazed out of my mind described my emotions. The headlines read: **Maximilian Blackstone the Billionaire Industrialist To Wed Socialite Jessica Beaumont in Las Vegas.**

When I gained my senses, I noticed a package placed at the door. I picked it up and looked at it. It was a box wrapped in beautiful floral paper, and it had a note attached. I opened the envelope and it read: ***You will probably need these items today. You never let me give you anything. Maybe you will now. Your Dom, Max.*** I wanted to take the package and throw it into the garbage, but my curiosity needed to be satisfied. I opened it and found a box of underwear and bras. Although I needed a change, I was pissed.

I reached for my smartphone and began texting.

Alex: Fuck u Max. Fuck u. Fuck u.

Max: Tell me when and where and I'll be there.

Alex: U will never get another chance, u dick.

Max: Never is a long time. U have such a potty mouth for such a pretty woman.

Alex: Since u r marrying Jessica, y don't we make it a double wedding. I'm going to accept Charles's proposal.

Max: U don't understand, Alex. I have a reason for this. U have no reason to marry St. John but to hurt me. Don't do it.

Alex: I know ur reason, u sex maniac.

Max: Maybe I'm one, but I'm urs.

I couldn't take it any longer; I knew I was on the precipice. I was one step from submitting to him and accepting anything he threw my way. I came to my senses, and realization took hold. I was playing Max's game, and he had just dealt an unforgivable blow. Reading about his upcoming marriage to Jessica had caused me to be weak, or maybe I didn't understand how horrific it was for him when I told him that I might marry Charles. He was winning this game, but I wasn't ready to submit to him. I wasn't ready to say that he had won, and I would do anything to have him and keep him.

I turned the phone off without answering the last text.

Chapter 12

Charles's face beamed when I accepted his marriage proposal, at the same time dismissing and ignoring Max's pleas. I smiled whenever Charles kissed me tenderly on my lips, feigning happiness like a stage actor. I got part of what I wanted—joint custody of my son. Max's hunched shoulders straightened when outside of court, in front of cameras, a reporter asked about the custody battle.

He didn't acknowledge defeat. He gestured, and said, "It's over. I'm going home to my son." But inside I knew that he had lost everything that he wanted. He hurried into his limo and drove away. Max had to bring Maxim to me in a month. The stipulation stated that Maxim could not be under Charles's roof unless we were married. That was Max's undoing. He bet wrong. He bet that I wouldn't marry Charles and that my threats were empty.

I turned over my bungalow to Crystal. Jonas had been in jail for three months, and still she continued to see Josh whenever he was in Seattle. I couldn't stand to see Crystal using Josh, and I couldn't face him. I disappeared into Charles's home on a secluded island in the Caribbean Sea.

Knowing that Max would do whatever it took to get Jonas free, and Joshua would be left out in the cold, I tried to distance myself from everyone. I agreed to be married at Charles's hideaway. It was an island with a large mansion perched high on a hill, surrounded by a small mountain range, and beautiful white sandy beaches. The only transportation was a jet to the neighboring island and a helicopter to Charles's estate.

The waves woke me each morning as they beat against the rocks, drowning out the sound of Max's voice in my head and the dreams of him in my body.

The sound of seagulls was a welcoming respite from the noise of the world and the awful news in the headlines. There was more going on in the world than my petty problems.

Sitting up and looking out of the window, I heard a soft knock at the door. It was my breakfast tray. I hadn't felt like myself in months. I ate very little food and slept more. Charles arranged for a doctor to see me and give me an exam, but that would be later today.

The maid tiptoed into the room. "Ms. Bishop, I have your breakfast and the newspaper."

"Leave it on the table. Thank you." It was hard having someone serve me, but I was getting used to it.

I reached for the toast and my eyes glanced at the newspaper headlines: **Jonas Blackstone Released; Jessica Beaumont Arrested for the Necktie Murder of San Francisco Heiress.**

My breath caught and I felt as if I was drowning, and I sat up straight. I couldn't open the paper fast enough to read it.

The article noted that Detective Blake Scotto and Maximilian Blackstone had arranged the taping of Jessica Beaumont, where she confessed to Max that she had killed the heiress, whom she had been in a sexual relationship with, and that she would have killed Alexander Bishop if Max had attempted to marry her.

That tape was inadmissible, but when interrogated by Blake and another detective, Jessica admitted that she and the heiress were indeed lovers and that they were into erotic asphyxiation, and it was "all a terrible accident."

The article further noted that Jonas's DNA was on the tie he had taken from Max's closet, but because the DNA of identical twins was the same, there was no differentiating Max's DNA from Jonas's.

The reporter continued that Jonas had masqueraded as Max. Jonas confessed to the crime to prevent Max from going to jail, because he wanted to protect Max and his son, Maxim.

I felt faint, so I lay down, and when I woke it was 1:00 p.m. The nurse informed me that the doctor was waiting. I hurried into the shower and dressed and met him in an office on the grounds of the estate. He asked me a series of questions concerning my health, and my mother's and father's health history. I informed him that I had been adopted and had not looked for my birth parents.

The nurse took samples of my blood to analyze.

It was a doctor's office with a lab. *That's how billionaires roll,* I thought. They had everything at their convenience. I was so caught up on not accepting a handout from Max that I missed something very important. He had money and things to give to me, only more than if I had fallen in love with a poor man. I happened to have fallen in love with a billionaire.

Blake was willing to spend his month's pay on taking me to dinner and a good bottle of wine. Only Max and Charles had much more, and they wanted to do the same. I accepted it from Charles, because Max made me angry. I was an ass of the highest form.

The doctor came back with the results of the test.

"You are a healthy twenty-three-year-old, and it is not unusual for you to be pregnant and still have a false menstrual cycle."

No. Pregnant? How? When? My mind revolved around the room, searching for the time it had occurred, and stopped on the day Max came to my house. It was not supposed to end with me having sex with him. Hell, it was not supposed to begin with him between my legs. I was celibate then—no men, and especially not Max. Too much had been happening, and I had forgotten to refill my prescription of birth control pills. I didn't have time to see my gynecologist, and my dentist, forget it. I hadn't seen him in six months, and with the coffee stains I looked a mess. I had finally gotten around to the dentist and now my smile was radiant for my wedding day.

Thank goodness for youth. Youth could mask most things in life. When you had ordinary looks you were as beautiful as a fresh flower to men of thirty, and in Charles's case, thirty-five. I had to tell Charles about my pregnancy. I couldn't keep that from him. But what was I going to do about Max? Would he believe that the child was his, or would I now have to prove that I had never had another man in my body but him? As horrible as I had been to Max, I wouldn't have blamed him if he walked away from me. *And Charles, what am I to say to him?*

I knew that if Max pissed me off, I would marry Charles out of spite. This whole situation was making me crazy, or was it my hormones driving me crazy and interfering with my thinking?

I left the doctor's office and walked from his cottage to the mansion, taking time to look at the beautiful flowers and inhale the wonderful scents. Reaching the side door, I entered and headed for the library. When Charles wasn't working in his office, I was sure to find him buried in a book. I quietly opened the door. He turned around.

"Oh it's you, Alex." He stood, laying the book and his glasses on the table. I turned in a circle to marvel at the vast number of books in his possession. His eyes followed my expression. "I can't bring myself to part with anything. I guess when I love something, I hoard it."

Well, that explained everything. He kept pictures of his wife and her clothes all through the house. He even had her room exactly as she had left it. And my surreal resemblance to her was shocking. I saw myself at thirty-five.

Looking up at her portrait, I said, "Charles, I have something to tell you."

"What is it?" He walked around his chair to stand in front of me, reaching for my hands and holding them. His gaze and his voice took a sexual tone. "You look ravishing today. You have a beautiful bloom on your face, like a flower that's ready to be plucked."

That is a word that I would never connect with this sedate and reserved man. Did I miss something? Did I overlook the sexual nature of this man?

"You need to sit, Charles."

"Only if you sit beside me," he said without expression, and he pointed to the place near him.

I drew a deep breath and then exhaled. His eyes watched mine and then settled on my mouth. He had this strange look I had seen on Max when Max's eyes landed on my mouth, then he declared that he wanted to fuck it. Clearly Charles would never say that, but I knew what he was thinking.

"I'm pregnant."

"Marvelous."

"What do you mean marvelous? I can't marry you now."

"If not me, who are you going to marry?"

"No one."

"Have you thought hard about your decision? What will Max say once he finds out?"

"I don't know. I just don't know."

"Now you will have two children by Max. You will never have the freedom that you crave. You are not rich, and you can't fight a man like that," he said matter-of-factly. "I promise you that I will put a stipulation in our agreement that if you marry me, you will have all the money you desire to make you independent of me and anyone, and if you discover that you do not want to be married to me, you are free to go, and I will pay for everything."

How can I turn down that offer? But my father once said, when something is too good to be true, it probably is. As usual I ignored his words and thought I had done the best for myself with what I had to deal with at this time.

I had forgotten that I was never good with contracts.

I hesitated. Then like a waterfall spilling its contents over a cliff, I said, "I'll marry you." Charles lightly kissed my forehead. I liked that he did not push himself on me. I liked that he was a gentleman, and I liked that he had patience.

He held my hand, and we sat together looking out into the sunset. Our gazes locked, and he gave a delicate smile, concealing a predatory expression of satisfaction that I had seen before on Max's face.

<hr>

MY WEDDING DAY WAS approaching. Saturday was the big day. This would be a life-altering occasion. I felt it when my father said that I had been adopted, I felt it when I met Max, I felt it when I found out I was pregnant, and I felt it when I first knew that Max had moved on and I would never have him again.

I tried calling and texting Max, but I received no answers. After our vows were said, then Max would deliver my son to me, and I would tell Max that he would have another child.

Informing Charles that I didn't want a large wedding had gone well. Because his friends knew his wife for a long time, they were none too happy with me marrying him. The decision to have a small wedding and invite a few family members proved easy on me and a delight. I was too nervous for a large celebration.

It was Friday. Crystal finally made it to Charles's island home. I was in my room sulking about Max not bringing Maxim. He'd conveniently dropped out of sight. He sent word by Josh that it might traumatize Maxim. In Max's words, "My son is too young to see his mother marry any man other than his father. It will confuse him."

I strolled down the winding stairs and heard voices in the library. The shouting was coming from Charles. Since I had never experienced that side of him, I thought it best that I didn't intrude. When the door opened, I slipped behind it. It was the doctor whom I had met earlier and had examined me, and who had said how remarkably I looked like Charles's wife.

"You need to tell her, Charles." I had no idea who the "her" was that he was referring to.

"I have no intention of doing that," he said, holding a brandy snifter in his hand and taking a large gulp.

"Someone should say something. Maybe I will."

"If you value your practice and clients, then you will not interfere in my affairs."

The doctor walked out of the room with Charles looking on. "Let me see you out."

"I have no problem seeing myself out." He paused, looking back. "Just remember what I said, Charles."

The doctor walked slowly out, heading for the nearest door to exit the mansion. Charles closed the double doors to the library. I hesitated with my fist to the door. I decided to knock, and Charles answered, "Come in."

"I overheard the doctor talking to you," I said, being secretive as if I knew what the conversation was about. Charles raised an eyebrow and took another drink, his face turning sullen. I added, "I didn't hear what he said, only that you 'need to tell her.'" I saw a look of relief wash over him and relax his face. His brow smoothed, and no longer did I see the lines break near his eyes. A wide smile crossed his mouth, and his impeccable white teeth made him appear more handsome.

Charles stood and faced me. He placed his arms around my shoulder, and all felt well. I was no longer worried and unhappy. He held me to him. I looked in his eyes, and I saw not erotic desire but a longing for something lost—the loss of his first love. And if I read it in his eyes, he certainly read it in mine.

Could Charles and I move past everything, especially Max and his wife, and learn to love each other? That would be the million-dollar question. He held me tight and gave me a soft kiss on my lips, which made me feel that it would not be long before I surrendered myself to him.

My need for Mr. Black had waned. I had not felt his arms in months, and I no longer dreamed of him entering and disappearing into my body.

<hr>

TODAY WAS THE DAY I would become Mrs. St. John. I had selected an eggshell-white, off-the-shoulder, satin Vera Wang gown. I didn't want a traditional veil and a church wedding. After all, I was pregnant with another man's child. We were to have a garden wedding near the beach. I had breakfast early in my room. Crystal was there with her happy self to be my maid of honor. It was good to see her smile again. I didn't have anyone but Crystal now.

My father at first refused to give me away when I told him of the new pregnancy. I knew it was because he didn't approve of Charles, and of not disclosing my pregnancy to Max, though my father gave no explanation. That was just the way he was. He told you once not to do something, and when questioned, he always said, "Because, I know best. I'm older than you. If you don't listen, you'll learn. You'll learn."

Max hadn't taken it well when I finally contacted him the day before the wedding. He said that he knew of the first Mrs. St. John, and that the only reason Charles was marrying me was because I resembled his first wife. I guessed that was never a reason to marry anyone, but coming from Max it sounded so perverse.

I looked out over the estate from my bedroom window and saw Charles riding his gray gelding on the beach. He came to the front door, and his groom took the horse. Charles appeared to be so calm. I admired him for that.

Looking at the clock, I saw that it was almost time for me to dress for our wedding. I shook violently as if something was very wrong. I wondered if I would see Max or Jonas, since they were not invited. A knock came at the door.

"It's time, Ms. Bishop," the housekeeper shouted nervously. "Everything is prepared, and you will be happy with the cake and the food. You need to take your shower. Someone will be in to do your hair, and then Crystal and I will help you dress."

When I exited the shower and wrapped a robe around my body, I walked into the living area to see a somber Crystal fidgeting with her hair, her left leg moving at the speed of light. "What is it this time?"

"Jonas and Josh are both coming to the wedding," Crystal said in a voice so low I had to lean in to hear her.

"Why would you invite Jonas? I told you to invite people in your family." I threw a pillow at her in anger. "I had to invite Joshua. You know that, Crystal. He's my best friend, and I need him for moral support."

"I'm dating both of them. I couldn't desert Jonas after all he has been through."

My eyes rolled, my head swung back, and I let out a loud sigh. "Didn't I tell you not to have them both hanging on? I told you to do something—anything—and this is what you did?"

Crystal mumbled something and walked into the closet to bring out my dress and shoes.

"I came to you because I thought you could tell me something, seeing that you have been dating two men, and not just any men, but rich men," Crystal said, sitting on the bed, hunched over, and looking at the floor.

I crossed the room and put my hand on her shoulder. "I understand how you feel, but when I decided that I was going to marry Charles, I let Max know, and I didn't waver. I didn't want Max to think that I might marry him. And besides, I had another reason for marrying Charles." But after thinking about what I was doing and had done, it didn't make sense anymore. I was marrying Charles to give me leverage with Max. I knew that I was using Charles, but if what Max said was true, he was using me as well. We were both getting what we wanted. *After all, we are adults*, as an arrogant, handsome, sexy billionaire once said.

"You have to make up your mind and live with your decisions," I said, trying to convince Crystal. *I hope I can live with mine*, I silently confessed.

"Is that what you're doing, Alex?" I glanced at Crystal. "Living with your decision?" she said, reading my expression.

"Yes. That's what you do when you are an adult. Live with your decisions and try not to hurt and get hurt. Nothing is guaranteed in life."

As our eyes met, the stylist knocked, and entered with the maid following. The maid had a smile on her face, and her eyes were bright. She was a young woman who appeared to love the sound of a wedding. Her eyes were full of Prince Charming and living happily ever after.

"It's your wedding day, Ms. Bishop. Soon you will be Mrs. St. John." She walked around the cluttered room, chatting and picking up shoes, clothes, and coffee cups.

After the stylist completed my hairstyle with a bun and curls framing my face, she worked on Crystal. I did my own makeup, which was not much. A little eye shadow here, a little lip gloss there, and a little blush, and I was done. With frayed nerves and shaky legs, I stepped into my dress. Crystal took more time with her makeup. She had been practicing for somebody's wedding since she was a little girl. Her false eyelashes brought out the beauty in her large eyes. She was a pretty girl and didn't know how to be dishonest.

That was why she sonfessed about Jonas and Joshua. Nevertheless, she wanted both and probably hoped I could help her keep them both. It was not meant to be, because they were two different men and they liked her very much, which was not good.

I knew how much Josh had wanted her, because he would call her when he was in Hong Kong. It had been very expensive to talk once a day, but he managed. No doubt he spent his bonus money to keep in contact with her, even after he tried to break it off. I think he heard the rumors about her and Jonas, and didn't want to look stupid in my eyes. He liked her and wanted to be more to her, but she was caught up with the bad boy and she couldn't shake that feeling, and neither could I.

I saw a change in Jonas whenever he was with Crystal. He was calm and pensive. He appeared to think before he did anything. He thoughtfully sent flowers and took her to dinner and brought her roses, something Mr. Black never did.

"It's time to go," Crystal said, looking at the clock.

"So soon?"

"What are you going to do, stay in here and have everyone come to the room? Remember, you have to live with your decisions," she said, eyeing me with a smirk.

Crystal knew the advice I dispensed was a load of shit. We both knew that I couldn't make up my mind and that Max had made it up for me when he texted me that he would marry soon.

Walking in a daze and missing the only man I had loved, I stumbled with every step down the stairs, but managed to make it through the garden doors. Charles had arranged to have beautiful flowers flown in from the nearby islands. Every color was represented. Flowers adorned the walkway and the centerpiece on each of the hundred tables, which were covered with fine white linen, under white tents.

My father took my arm. He stated that he couldn't desert me. Gazing at me, he said, "You are beautiful." I heard a traditional wedding ballad, and saw my mother on the front row crying, and standing on the stage of the gazebo was Charles in his black tux with a boutonniere in his buttonhole.

I couldn't help thinking, *Let's get this over with*. It was a slow walk to meet the man I would be with for the rest of my life. It was a slow walk to be with a man I didn't love. It was a slow walk to make promises I couldn't keep.

Blinded by how handsome Charles was standing in his black tux, I imagined that he was Mr. Black. How I missed that gorgeous, domineering, jealous man. Standing alongside of Charles was his best man, the doctor who had said, "Tell her." He knew Charles's secret. I didn't know they were close friends.

My father in his black suit, a concerned look on his face, stepped aside and released my hand to Charles. There was a somber look on my father's face—the kind of look that made the hair rise on my neck. Maybe he knew something too. Facing the minister, he began the ceremony. As I looked into the minister's eyes, they changed, and his voice became louder, and his words began to speed up.

━━━━●━━━━

A SUDDEN ROAR CAME from the guests, and then the noise died down. I thought it was a squirrel that had scampered across the lawn, or a seabird taking a shot at the fancy hats the women were wearing. The minister continued, and said, "If anyone should say why these two should not be married, let them speak..."

"I know why."

"What?"

I turned to see Max bounding from the arms of security guards, and Jonas standing ready to assist his brother. "Let him speak," Jonas said. Jonas had grown a slight beard and cut his hair in a buzz cut. I hardly recognized him.

Max stood on the carpet midway to the gazebo. The guards came behind him and grabbed both arms. Charles's eyes narrowed at me.

"I want to hear what he has to say, and then we will get on with the wedding," I said, trying to hold back my excitement of seeing Max break through a throng of security guards to stop my wedding.

My eyes held Max's, and he stood in front of me and Charles. I saw tears pool in his green eyes, when he stated, "I can't live without you. I need you. We need you to make our family whole again. Don't do this, Alex."

"Those words were touching, but are you finished so I can get on with my wedding?" Charles said, perturbed. His steely eyes met the soft warmth of Max's tear-drenched face.

Max's face hardened at the sound of Charles's arrogant words. His tears dried with a brush of the back of his sleeve.

"No, I haven't begun. If you don't want the world to hear this, then you had better postpone this ceremony, and you and Alex meet me in the library, so we can talk. That is, without your bodyguards."

I gazed at Charles with puzzlement. His eyes darted away from mine, and he waved for the microphone. "There will be a brief pause in the wedding ceremony for me to address the intruder who has chosen this time to disrupt my wedding. Please, have some champagne and food while you wait." Charles gave a broad smile as if he was in charge of everything and that I should not worry.

The guests mumbled to one another, and then with smiles they rose and were directed by men dressed in black suits with white shirts and white gloves to a tent for food and drinks.

I wasn't worried. I wanted to see my Mr. Black, even if it was just for a moment. Crystal trailed behind me and cast a glance at Josh, who sat to the left, and Jonas, who sat on the right facing the gazebo. Then Josh and Jonas stared seriously at each other. I hoped they would resolve their problems, because mine were immediate and complicated.

Heading to the library, I stopped and turned. "Crystal, you can't come in here. This is between Max, Charles, and myself." She dropped the train of my gown and showed me her crossed fingers. She was always wishing me good luck, and I gave her one back, because she would need it with Jonas. Josh, however, went with the flow. He was easy to like, he was easy to love, and he would be easy to say goodbye to if she chose that route.

I entered the library, where a nervous Max paced up and down the Oriental rug, holding a cigar in his hand. He stopped in his tracks, catching a glimpse of our faces, and stated, "Charles, I took this opportunity to enjoy one of your Cuban cigars." He set it on a holder and then he shoved his hands in his pockets. Maybe that was to conceal the shaking of his hands, but his voice showed no loss of control, even as he was out of his element and on Charles's turf.

However, I knew Max. His body language suggested that it was a matter of life or death for him.

"What is it, Max? Haven't you done enough damage to me?"

"It's not what you think, sweetheart."

"Don't refer to her as your sweetheart," Charles said, lowering his voice. He continued, "She is soon to be my wife. Do you understand?"

"That is a matter of opinion," Max said, reaching for his cigar and taking a pull on it, turning his head to his right, and blowing out the smoke.

"Can you both stop this?" I said, standing between them. "Max, tell me what is so urgent that you couldn't say it in front of our guests." Max's eyes softened, and his face appeared sad. He just stared into my eyes for a long minute.

"Well, get on with it, man," Charles interrupted.

Max's face and voice reacted to Charles. "How do I say this delicately?" He took another pull on the cigar as Charles and I waited.

"Use your usual bull-in-the-china-shop approach," I interrupted. "We are all adults."

"You are the daughter of St. John's late wife," he blurted out.

I wanted to faint. I wanted to cry, but most of all I wanted to die. I didn't want to hear this from Max. What I had overheard at the door of the library was about me. "You have to tell her, Charles," the doctor had said to Charles in the library.

I switched my attention to Charles. "Is this true? Why didn't you tell me, Charles?" I gazed at him with concentrated loathing. "Are you my father?"

"You're not my daughter. I didn't need to tell you, because I'm not your father."

"I deserved to know who my mother was. You could have said something."

"I wanted to, Alex. But I needed you, and I thought that you would reject me. I have nothing to say except that I'm sorry."

I looked at Charles. Exhaustion overwhelmed me. "What happened? Why did she put me up for adoption?"

"She had gotten pregnant in her last year of high school by a football jock. I was off to college, and we were to be married after I had graduated and received my inheritance. I didn't find out about you until we were married. We tried to have a child of our own, but she was unable to conceive. We tried to find you, and when we did, you were a teenager, so we paid for your living expenses and college, making sure you wanted for nothing. When your mother died, I lost track of you, and then you showed up at my hotel looking for a job.

"It was remarkable how much you looked like my wife—your mother—and I began to investigate, and that's when I discovered that you and Maximilian were lovers, and you were Anna's daughter. It was innocent at first, but then it was amazing how much you and she were alike. I began to relive my life again through you."

I pulled away.

Remembering how I cared for this man, I walked back to him. I passed my hand along his jaw. He held it and brought my hand to his mouth, and then, turning the palm to his lips, he lowered his head and kissed it. I turned to face Max, knowing that I had made a big mistake and hoping he would forgive me.

"Don't leave me, Alex. I need you," Charles cried out as I ran to Max and buried my head into his chest.

"I have three people who need me more. You have had your life and love. I need to have my love and my memories too." I turned away, walking with my head lowered, clutching Max's hand. He led me through the doors of Charles's mansion, where he had a limo waiting in front. We were silent, and I would not release his hand. I needed the security of Max.

Charles stood at his front door, holding back his tears, and said, "If Max is foolish enough to let you get away, I'll be waiting."

We slipped into the limo with Max still holding my hand tight.

Leaning close, I lay my head against his chest, glancing up at him in silence. My thoughts could be read in my eyes. *What a beautiful, sexy man I have. He must be a saint to put up with a spoiled brat like me.*

———◦———

IT HAD BEEN A LONG, exhausting day and night. When I woke, Max was carrying me from his private jet to his limo. It was a blur. All I remembered was waking to the sound of rain. I peeped out of the panoramic windows, which were devoid of curtains, and saw tall pine trees. Through the trees sunlight stole into the bedroom, and I knew we were in Montana. "Hi there, sleepyhead. How long are you going to lie there?" Max said, leaning against the doorframe from the sitting area to his bedroom. "I have a camping trip planned."

I smiled and said, "I hope it's not today and there are no bugs. You know how I hate bugs."

"I can't promise you that there will be no bugs. There will be one, and that's me. And no, it's not today." He sat on the edge of the bed and crawled into it. "I love you, Alex. When can we marry and make it legal? Because what I plan to do to you in bed isn't legal in some states." He gave a wink. The glint in Max's eyes made me hot. My hands reached under his pajama top and trailed down his chest.

"You have been working out, I see." My head lowered to his chest, and I kissed each muscle. Then my lips eased around his nipple, and I bit one hard. He reached for my head and gently gathered a handful of hair, pulling it back and raising my face to his.

"You have been holding out on me," he said with his dimples carving vertical lines into each side of his jaw. "I think we should enter into another contract. You have skills you have been holding back," he said, showing a slanted smile.

My Mr. Black had finally become my Prince Charming who slayed the dragons and rescued me, and took me to his castle.

"Whenever and wherever you want, I'm open to anything."

"Anything?" he said with a wicked grin. "Well, it's been some time, and I need to try you out first. You're like one of my sports cars, sleek and beautiful, but a little fragile. I need to know how you handle around the curves." He placed his hands on my hips, caressing them and causing my skin to tingle.

His hands moving slowly, making love to my clit, he inserted his finger into my vagina. His sinful jade eyes followed my nipples as they rose when he placed two fingers in me, causing arousal of the basest kind, where I would let him tie me up and spank me, and I would satisfy him with whatever he desired all night, until he had sated his needs.

He nipped at my neck, his mouth and tongue tickling my underarms. His lips found mine, and my mouth opened wide, waiting for his tongue to find its way, and then devouring it. "I need a closer inspection," he said, raising his head. His mouth sucked my nipples until they peaked with wanton desire, then he moved his lips over my stomach.

Stopping him with my finger placed in front of his lips, I looked down on him. "I have to tell you something first."

"I hope you haven't become celibate, because I can't wait to feel the inside of you and taste your sweet pussy."

I missed his not-so-delicate way of expressing his love for me.

"I'm... I'm pregnant." His eyes widened and he began to laugh.

"When were you going to tell me?"

"Soon," I said, lowering my eyes.

His brow narrowed and furrowed. "You know you have been a bad girl, and if you weren't with child, I would place you over my knee and use these large hands to paddle your beautiful ass." He raised his hands, placed them on my stomach, and caressed it lovingly. He didn't ask whose child; somehow he knew. But most of all he knew that I could never be unfaithful to him, and he had never been to me.

Our bond was that deep.

"I need you so bad. I want to have your dick inside me."

"I don't think I should," he said, excited that I was making the advances. "You know I'm not that kind of man."

"What kind are you?"

"The kind that will not take advantage of a damsel in distress, but you look like a beautiful innocent flower." He bit my nipple. "And I intend to enjoy the beauty of your petals before I pluck them."

"It's safe." I pulled him to me and placed his hands between my legs. "Now do what you do best, Mr. Black." His hands moved around in a circle with his fingers teasing my bud until it stood hard.

"It's ripe for the taking," he announced. He eased between my legs, and his tongue brushed up and down until his mouth covered my bud. He licked me slowly, then quickly. Then, he nibbled it softly and began to suck it, until I screamed, "I'm coming."

When I uttered those words, he reached for my breasts and fingered each nipple, and then like a vise his fingers pinched them, until I became so aroused that I had my second orgasm.

I fell back against the pillow, breathing hard, and shouting, "Max, Max, I want more."

He stood, untied the string to his pajama bottoms, and let them drop. Stepping out of them, he faced me with his dick hard and erect. He inched onto the bed and straddled me. As he looked down, my body ached from the absence of him inside me. He lived inside of my body as I lived for his touch.

His greedy mouth and hands moved quietly and patiently, until his mouth found my mound. My legs parted, waiting for him to shove his hard shaft into my greedy vagina. Every so often he glanced up, focusing on my belly, which carried his child, but he found himself hesitating. I knew that he didn't want to hurt me, but we needed each other like the fish needed the oceans and the oceans needed water.

"You won't hurt me." I anticipated his thoughts. I rose and pushed him backward and hungrily forced his penis into my mouth. His pulse beat fast, and the ridges of my lips felt the motion. I placed my hand around his penis and pulled his erection from my mouth and slid it around my lips, and without any hands, my mouth grasped to hold onto it. I worked my mouth up and down and used my hands to caress his hard thighs.

Breathless, he said, "Oh, you do have skills."

Sucking his shaft, I held on to his hard buttocks and helped him lean it into my mouth. The upward motion of his body excited me, and I began moving with him. Up and down he thrust his hard shaft forward, and I took all of it. It was a feeling I hadn't had in some time. It was wonderful, giving and controlling. The feeling was long forgotten, but once it occurred, it was like riding a bike; you would never forget how.

"What are you doing to me? I can't come now. Don't make me come, Alex. I want to savor all of this." I reached around and caressed his hard ass, pressing my nails into each cheek, and dragging them down until skin broke.

I felt come ease out of his body, and my jaws tightened around his dick. He let out a hard groan. "I'm coming, Alex. But I'm not satisfied, and I know that you're not." He faced me, and with his come easing down my mouth, he wiped it away with the sheet and he kissed me.

As I looked into his eyes, he inserted his penis into my vagina. His swollen dick felt as if it rose into my chest. With a slow rhythm he thrust deeper. I tightened my legs around his waist and rode his body, sinking my mound above his and grinding on it, until I felt where his dick began and ended.

Exhausted, he fell into my arms, reaching for my swollen breasts, and softly his tongue massaged my tips, making them large. He glanced at me. "I'd better enjoy them now, because soon I will have to share them. I don't like to share the things I love with anyone, but I will make an exception this time," he stated with a gleam in his eyes. I could see my body fading into the dark hue of his irises. He cupped my breasts with his hands and lowered his mouth to my tits and sucked them ever so carefully. My vagina heated to its boiling point, and I felt the warmth of fluid release as I saw Max's penis rise and pulsate.

Max dissolved into a deep sleep with his head lying in the middle of my breasts.

———◈———

ALEX WOKE THE NEXT morning expecting Max to have disappeared, but he was lying close behind her, nuzzling her body. His arms draped over her stomach, and his nose lay in her hair. In his sleep, his head moved to her ear as he placed a small kiss on her neck, and his hand caressed her stomach. She placed her hand over his, and he felt the warmth of it and opened his eyes.

Compelled by his love and the desires he harbored for Alex, he touched her face, her hair, her breasts, and her stomach. She turned, facing him, and Max's finger made a circular motion around her lips, as if his finger was a brush and he would paint a picture. Each touch he made with his fingertips on the ridges of her plump lips caused a rise in his manhood.

A sound from her smartphone indicated that she had an e-mail. "Go ahead, Alex. Read your e-mails. I need to take a shower, and then we can resume our honeymoon." He sat with his back to Alex, his body naked and his legs dangling on the floor.

Alex smiled, trailing kisses across Max's back. "We aren't married yet."

Max stepped from under the covers. His body overexcited and his permanent erection still prominent, he stood facing her.

"You know you need to do something with that," she said, pointing to his erection. Max headed back to the bed. "No. Go." Alex waved him on. "The commercials said that if you have an erection for over four hours, then you need to see a doctor." They both laughed, and Max entered the shower.

Alex opened the text. It was a message from Charles. She sighed. "What now?"

Charles: Alex. I know u r happy. I don't know how to make up for what I put u through with my selfish behavior. Please, forgive me.

There was another text shortly after, and Max exited the shower with his hair wet and a white towel hooked around his waist. He saw the pain on Alex's face. "What's wrong?"

"Nothing. What could be wrong? I have never been this happy," she said, holding her now prominent belly with one hand and the phone in the other. She didn't want to hide anything from Max. "There are a few texts from Charles, and I'm going to read them." She patted the indent where his body had lain. Max sat on the side of her and gazed at the screen.

Charles: Alex. I have ur mother's jewelry and I want u to have them for ur daughter. There is also her will. She left everything to u.

They each glared at the other, and Alex blurted out, "A will?"

Max shouted, "No. Charles did that on purpose."

The farther away Charles appeared to be in Alex's life, the closer he inched.

Next

Book 4 (Black Tie Affair) Published and next in the series of 10 books.

Blog: http://www.rachel-e-rice.com

Don't miss out!

Visit the website below and you can sign up to receive emails whenever Rachel E Rice publishes a new book. There's no charge and no obligation.

https://books2read.com/r/B-A-ASU-AJZC

BOOKS 2 READ

Connecting independent readers to independent writers.

Did you love *Submission To Black*? Then you should read *One Desire*[1] by Rachel E Rice!

When Tyler Burns graduates from a prep school in New Jersey and is the valedictorian of her prestigious high school, she assumes that her working-class background will take her only so far. And it probably would have gotten her a working-class stiff like her father, but she gets more than she expects when she meets Brandon Charles, a Princeton graduate, hot as the noon-day sun, with his blue-green eyes, sexy good looks, and a body to bring her to her knees. It's no wonder he's engaged, and he's expected to marry within a week.

Tyler accepts a ride home with Brandon from the frat party, never intending to end up in his bed at his estate, but she does. And if things can't get worse it does. She stays with him for a week, and most of the

---

1. https://books2read.com/u/m2RNRm

2. https://books2read.com/u/m2RNRm

week is spent in bed. He promises her he will return once he calls off the wedding. And she believes him and waits for him, but he never returns that night, or the next, or the next.

Five years later, she has graduated from college, when Brandon strolls back into her life in a restaurant with a beautiful girl, and Tyler is their waitress.

Read more at www.rachel-e-rice.com.

Also by Rachel E Rice

Blackstone
The Incredible Mr. Black
Blackstone Complete 10 Books Dark Romance Series
Temptation In Black
Blackstone Series 4 Books Box Set
Submission To Black
Black Tie Affair
The Incredible Mr. Black Box Set
Mourning Becomes Black
Fade To Black
Back to Black
Black Tide
Black Swan
Blackout
Blackstone Series 6 Books Box Set

I Am The Night
I Am The Night

Insatiable

Insatiable: The Lone Werewolf finds his mate
Insatiable: A Werewolf's Hunger
Insatiable: A Werewolf's Wedding
Insatiable: The Werewolves' Challenge
Hunter's Moon
Moon Tide
Moon Rapture

Insatiable Werewolf Series
A Bride For A Werewolf: The Beginning
Thorn in Moonscape
Insatiable: Damon in Moonscape
A Werewolf's Passion
Moonscape Box Set

Night
I Am First Night
I Am Last Night

Obsession
Obsession: Warm Bodies,Cold Hearts
Naked Obsession
Burning Obsession

Seduction
Seduced By An Earl

The Captain
The Captain and The Virgin

The Soul of A Vampire
Soul of A Vampire
Soul of A Vampire Book 2
Soul of A Vampire Book 3

To kill a vampire
To Kill a Vampire
To Kill A Vampire
To Kill A Vampire

Standalone
Finding Summer
One Desire
Insatiable Box Set: Books 1-4
Hunter's Moon Box Set
Hunter's Moon Insatiable Series
Insatiable: Tracker #8
Soul of A Vampire Box Set
The Complete Insatiable Werewolf Bundle
The Complete Insatiable Werewolf Bundle
I Am The Night Box Set
A Vampire Bundle
A Vampire Bundle

I Am The Night Box Set
To Kill A Vampire Boxset
To kill A Vampire Boxset
A Complete Vampire Bundle

Watch for more at www.rachel-e-rice.com.

About the Author

Rachel E. Rice enjoys writing in different genres. As an Indie author she explores genres to find her voice. She has written contemporary romance, erotic romance, new adult, historical and science fiction.

When she's not writing she is reading poetry. She has a BA and is a member of Romance Writers of America.

Read more at www.rachel-e-rice.com.